BE GOOD *a novel by* STACEY MAY FOWLES

TIGHTROPE BOOKS
2007

BE
GOOD

a novel by
stacey may fowles

Canada Council   Conseil des Arts
for the Arts   du Canada

ONTARIO ARTS COUNCIL
CONSEIL DES ARTS DE L'ONTARIO

toronto**arts**council
An arm's length body of the City of Toronto

Tightrope Books
17 Greyton Crescent
Toronto, Ontario
Canada M6E 2G1
www.tightropebooks.com

EDITOR: Ari Berger
COPY EDITOR: Shirarose Wilensky
COVER DESIGN + PHOTO: Spencer Saunders
AUTHOR PHOTO: R. Kelly Clipperton
TYPESETTING: Carleton Wilson

Produced with the support of the Canada Council for the Arts, the Ontario Arts Council and the City of Toronto through the Toronto Arts Council.

PRINTED IN CANADA

LIBRARY AND ARCHIVES CANADA CATALOGUING IN PUBLICATION

Fowles, Stacey May

Be good / Stacey May Fowles.

ISBN 978-0-9783351-0-6

I. Title.

PS8611.O877B4 2007   C813'.6   C2007-904394-1

For my mother and father,
who taught me to be good even when the world was not.

"...not only have I always had trouble distinguishing between what happened and what merely might have happened, but I remain unconvinced that the distinction, for my purposes, matters."

– Joan Didion, *On Keeping a Notebook*

"According to neurobiologist Gerald Edelman, there are ten billion neurons in the human cerebral cortex, and more potential connections between those neurons than there are subatomic particles in the entire estimated physical universe. It is a system of near-infinite complexity, a system that seems designed for revision as much as for replication, and revision unquestionably occurs."

– John Daniel, *The Province of Personal Narrative*

"Go tell that long tongue liar
Go and tell that midnight rider
Tell the rambler,
The gambler,
The back biter
Tell 'em that God's gonna cut 'em down
Tell 'em that God's gonna cut 'em down."

– Johnny Cash, "God's Gonna Cut You Down"

VANCOUVER

You could write about France, but you don't know France.
You know absolutely nothing about France. Nothing at all.
You know forty days of rain and infidelity and Starbucks.
You know regret and the fluorescent lights of the twenty-four
*   hour 7-Eleven on Granville Street.*
No France.
Only postcards from France.

Prologue

MORGAN

Encoding *refers to the initial perception and registration of information.* Storage *is the retention of encoded information over time.* Retrieval *refers to the processes involved in using stored information.*

MY MOTHER (ALWAYS TACTLESS and almost always drunk) says in a long distance call from Toronto to Montreal, "Write it down, honey."

A pack a day smoker, a functional alcoholic, a broken woman, her insides riddled with disease, her left breast and her uterus removed, always telling me to write it down, as if a script has some grand importance and validity, capable of overshadowing reality.

My reality. Her reality.

"Write it down, honey."

And I remember they (whoever *they* are) always said, "Let your reader know where you are coming from and where you are going. Let them know where the end is. Be succinct. Clarify."

They told me there had to be a beginning, a middle and an end to things, even if you are (as I am) speaking from far beyond and far before the end. When you are naïve and apt to believe, you truly depend on the notion that there is a clear beginning, middle and end.

That there is a truth and a progression among all these recollections.

Perhaps I am not so apt to believe in that kind of truth. I believe that things are much better when broken into pieces, because the whole is deceptive at best.

My past is a carefully linked chain of lies and my present is nothing more than the sparkle of swept dust.

Chapter 01

HANNAH

". . . IT'S THE HEAT," Finn says.

Which is funny because the climate is considerably less manic here, less drastic, less extreme, like the people and their lack of panic every day. It's always cool here, so the heat can't be the reason. It's probably the fact that I'm standing over him day in and day out, a little match girl begging for attention like coins, a girl with bad skin to match her bad temperament and bad posture. He can't tell me it's just the heat that makes him ridiculously impossible to be around except when we're fucking, which is rare right now because I can't be touched without getting all panicked and fidgety. I never come anyway.

So it can't be the heat.

I imagine I am bohemian, which is ridiculous because my Daddy co-signed on my line of credit and I can't handle my weed. I wanted to have a collection of vintage vinyl in a goldenrod and muted lime loft apartment, but I don't own a record player and my landlord insists on standard-issue eggshell sanatorium white for my overpriced shoebox cell. I was the centre of something once, but now I have lost that temporary stardom. When I daydream I fantasize that someone will steal me away and make me interesting, like those two kidnapped teenage girls made over on the cover of *People* magazine. I'm sure they got their own cosmetic contracts as soon as they were released from the trunk of that car.

I am broke. I am average. There is a piece of me missing. And it's named Morgan.

Yesterday I watched a homeless man shoplift a can of processed ham from the shelf of the Granville Street 7-Eleven. He looked up at me as he stuffed it into the pocket of his heavy grey overcoat and shot me a yellowed checkerboard grin. I averted my gaze into my Styrofoam coffee cup and tore open a sugar packet, thinking, "What the fuck am I doing here?"

Thank Heaven for 7-Eleven, the sugar packet read.

Every day I wake up in this town I ask myself, "What the fuck am I doing here?"

Despite what the glossy travel brochures say, this town is actually full of junkies, skinny people with hollow faces, seething desperation. And then there are mountains and water and packed skyscapes and skyscrapers beyond anything I have ever seen. Mothers with pocked skin like sandpaper and outdated shag haircuts telling their Ritalin-ridden children, "Mommy's a recovering addict, honey." All the pretty soy milk-fed girls, their flesh curving, puckering, fighting to escape obnoxiously fluorescent bikinis as they skip stones on salt water, water I had never before tasted.

My apartment building is full of miserable single men in their late thirties, clutching their laundry, too nervous to look me in the eye when I say hello in the elevator.

In downtown Vancouver everything's in hyper-contrast, over-exposed like bad high school art class photographs, while the uniform grey of constant rain makes the blacks and whites of emotional chaos completely disappear.

There is this very real feeling that I don't belong in the aromatherapy, herbal remedy wilderness that is the exoskeleton of this shiny glass town. They all said, "Oh it's so beautiful there," but the beautiful ugliness of it all only makes me feel uglier. Perhaps this is because my version of beauty was always the dirty, aging kind, like too much dust on a leather-bound tome. I suppose I thought this town would detoxify me, clean me out like a colonic, but so far I've just managed to smoke more, eat less, and break out in an anxiety rash.

It's so antiseptically clean here, so smog free, it's making me sick.

Morgan said it would take a mere two weeks for me to freak out and blow all my money on the first flight east. It's been eight weeks, and almost all of my money is blown on things other than a plane ticket, but her prediction was not entirely wrong. My form of freaking out involved me perfecting the art of baking peach and blueberry pies for Finn and devising the most effective method of cleaning the scum from an already immaculately clean bathtub.

When my mother found out about my sudden domesticity she worried to the point of tears and begged me to do what Morgan figured I would do anyway.

"I'll send you air mail from Europe, honey. *Air mail,*" Morgan said to me on the phone during the first call I had gotten from her after three long weeks of being out west.

She said it as if she didn't realize that she didn't need to go to Europe, as if she didn't know Montreal was already far enough away for me to receive *air mail*. She said it as if my life was mundane enough that a piece of cardstock with the Eiffel Tower printed on it would have any meaning to me.

A terminally blonde girl at one of my many unsuccessful job interviews said, "People from the east always hate it here. They go back as soon as the rainy season hits."

"I thought we were in the rainy season already."

She laughed as if the thought of my inevitable failure and disappointment amused her beyond belief.

When Finn went west before me six months ago I was left in Montreal smoking a cigarette, holding a suddenly adopted potted plant, standing on a street corner in the snow while the car pulled away. Like I was in some bad eighties teen movie, some John Hughes manufactured joke made just for me.

The city where we now live is full of crazed narcotic faces and shiny glass skyscrapers, each one appearing to be eaten out, gnawed at, exposed like prisoners stripped and deloused before an eternity of entrapment. Beyond those transparent towers are majestic mountains capped in heavy clouds, infinite reflections back and forth in the buildings like a fun house in an amusement park.

There was no rain when I was here in February to decide whether leaving the frozen east behind was the right decision in my post-educational career crisis. I wondered if the temporarily clear skies were inviting me to run west, despite everything. Of course, those same skies opened wide the very day I arrived to stay, and all the open dumpsters breathed a heavy, greasy sigh to mock me. All these strange glass towers and all this rain and waiting, every day, for a man who doesn't love me to get home late from work and eat a slice of blueberry pie.

When I came west I wanted – no – was going to be the girl at the Sunday farmer's market who just had an orgasm in a sun-drenched four-poster bed a few hours before. I wanted to be the iconic girl in Vargas' drawings of pin-up princesses who wear silk panties and play with kittens all day long. The kind of girl that you can tell never wears a bra under that lemon yellow dress, the one that exposes the upper portion of her left breast as she leans in to examine some vine-ripened tomatoes. You just know she's got vanilla scented candles and a magazine rack full of art periodicals in her studio apartment with huge bay windows, exposed brick and a view of the ocean. Men buy her stuff. She grows fresh herbs on her kitchen windowsill. She gets out of bed when she wants without the piercing guilt that she is disappointing someone.

When I imagined myself in silk panties examining tomatoes I didn't, of course, factor in my own personal poverty, lack of orgasms and genetic penchant for depression.

My bachelor apartment looks out over rows and rows of other apartments, each of their inhabitants dreaming their dreams of the west, dreaming that one day they will finally see the ocean and loathing me because my building is the reason they cannot.

Sometimes I watch beautiful Finn sleep in that dopey, open-mouthed way he does, and I realize that he is the only real reason I can pinpoint when faced with the question of why I am here, a question that I have been desperately avoiding. He occasionally lets me have what he calls my "juvenile lesbian tendencies" and takes me for sushi when it's my only solace, but he can't tell me he loves me, and he refuses to cohabitate with me, despite the fact that I followed him here and am now forced to eat free samples at the upscale supermarket to save money.

It is true that his home has become mine. This fact stretches him beyond his limits, pushes his boundaries, but I stretch and push because my tiny one room apartment feels like a prison, a prison I pay for and decorate with a past I yearn to dive back into. I am consumed by a loneliness so large it won't be assuaged with fifties love ballads or extended bubble baths or baking pies.

". . . it's the heat," he says, scratching at his thinning hair and staring at the television as Alex Trebek reveals the Double Jeopardy question.

So I know, now more than I ever have, that it can't just be the heat. I know this because there is no heat. There is no warmth here at all.

I will make it through the year, and I know that Morgan

would say that I won't, primarily because Morgan always disagrees with me, especially now with her new found wisdom of an older boyfriend and world travelling on his dime. Fuck her and her postcards from Paris. Like Finn, she can't say *I love you* either, and I would have done anything to hear those words come out of her overly painted red mouth. Not that she'd ever admit it, but I used to be her mother, holding her head in my lap while she cried and bled and complained. Now I'm just another name on her international mailing list.

All I can do not to suffer the inevitable is numb myself to the truth until every last fidgeting doubt shuffles away on reluctant feet, out the exit door of my already cramped skull.

Chapter 02

POSTCARD

Hannah,
After a stop in Paris I headed down to St. Jean de Luz
to spend a few days taking it easy.
I leave tonight for Madrid.
After that down to Malaga and Morocco.
Hope you're well.
Be Good.

Chapter 03

MORGAN

Whenever people successfully recall a prior experience, they must have encoded, stored *and* retrieved *information about the experience.*

HERE'S THE WAY IT GOES, the way it always goes, and there's no disputing it, so don't even try:

Life is a series of painful, tragic, unbearable events. Even the pleasurable moments have a distinct ache to them because you know damn well that they are fleeting, and it is best simply to avoid them because they make life's painful trajectory infinitely harder to bear. And when you wake up one morning and feel the itch of bliss creep over you, you must realize that it is merely the marker that starts the path towards pain, because all the gain will merely become a loss in the end.

Better to have gained nothing than to have lost everything.

So I have made the following rules, having written them on a cocktail napkin at some ungodly hour, under the influence, while a stranger fondled my left knee:

1) Don't kiss the gorgeous foreign blue-eyed boys (and gorgeous foreign blue-eyed boys are plentiful in Montreal, so the temptation is endless). Don't kiss them on patios, at parties or at bars, despite the intake of too much cheap champagne and too much cheap festive cheer.

2) Don't be tricked into taking off your shoes and dancing with an amorous companion in a public fountain one moonlit night in July. (I did that once and it proved to be a deceptive activity.)

3) And when a boy tells you he's leaving don't, by any means, ask him to stay, because he just might, and the only thing that'll leave you with is a distinct and pervasive fear of the open door.

I know what type of girl I am. I am the type of girl men cheat on their girlfriends and wives with. I am the type of girl that men court before they meet the girl they spend the rest of their lives with. I am an escape, a vacation from real love, an affectionately nicknamed *firecracker*.

"Morgan, you're so much *fun*," they'd say when they were done.

Having said that, it doesn't faze me, pain me or cripple me. I am happy to live on the whore side of the virgin/whore complex, and I take a strange pride in the fact that I am the one who allows girls with cherry lip gloss and firm morals to find a love that only really exists in reaction to me. I just let their future husbands suckle as long as they need to, and then I let them go when they want to.

Hannah the virgin and Morgan the whore.

Finn suckled too before he found Hannah, and I kept that to myself as she applied cherry lip gloss and wrote her first name connected to his last name in the margins of her notebooks.

I am not a caregiver and I am not a caretaker. I get late night phone calls and drunken invitations. I kiss strangers. No one will ever write a love song for me, and I will never listen to a love song and think of someone else.

Can't have it, then I don't want it.

I am going through the filthiest of motions and I am enjoying them, pure and simple.

Chapter 04

HANNAH

WHEN I FIRST MET Morgan in the dead of yet another Montreal winter I thought she was the most beautiful living creature I had ever seen in my life. I wanted to reach out and touch her to confirm that she was real.

Of course, I also felt that way about Finn when I first saw him at an Old Port party at the end of that year's summer, but the first time I saw him I drank too many Cape Cods, and with Morgan I was stone cold sober in a lecture hall on the third floor of the visual arts building.

Morgan was not her real name, but no one ever learned the real one, or much of anything else about her. I was sure her name was Elizabeth or Jane or something equally suburban. Everything about Morgan was as made up as her name, her life a carefully linked chain of half-truths and full un-truths.

She had a porcelain, ethereal quality about her: raven black hair and alabaster skin so pale it was almost transparent. She was all overdone pale moody cool and pouty dark-eyed disinterest. She sat next to me during the first day of a second-semester art history class, and she was the only one who didn't look completely sickly and hung-over post-Christmas vacation in the buzzing flicker of the fluorescent-lit classroom.

I felt immediately as if I had been waiting all my life for her to appear.

Morgan always smelled like grape Bubblicious and was unusually tall, resulting in a folded frame posture that was actually worse than mine, a fact that only made her more endearing to me. Her body was all Bettie Page burlesque, her bra strap always exposed from beneath a scissor-cropped t-shirt and her flesh squeezing out from beneath the strap's red elastic pull. She stomped around like an eight-year-old boy who had consumed too much sugar and was in desperate need of a time-out.

Morgan also had a completely undefined ethnicity about her, and, as I later discovered, she herself didn't know her origins except that her mother was a recovering addict who dumped her in the lobby of an adoption agency. She told me she had been found in an orange crate, wrapped in torn out comic book pages.

"Pay attention to me," she seemed to scream with every bullshit story.

I drew countless portraits of her and pasted them into my ever-fattening scrapbook. I took hundreds of photographs of her and catalogued them by date, symptomatic of the fact that I feared she would simply disappear and I would have no tangible proof that she had ever existed.

Morgan had even had a brief stint as a childhood beauty pageant contestant, care of her hard-drinking, overbearing yet emotionally distant suburban stay-at-home mother, and sometimes she would treat me to brief filmic images of her on damaged videotape as a pink-cheeked and blonde seven-year-old on parade.

When I first saw her during that lecture, she was drawing images of butterflies and soft-core porn in her perfume-scented notebook. She once told me that when she came she saw images of lotus flowers blooming. I didn't even know what lotus flowers looked like, and I certainly didn't come enough to have any visions to associate. It was only natural that a girl like Morgan, a girl so unlike me, would be multi-orgasmic.

Credit card debt collectors were constantly hunting her, but she always found a way to purchase a designer dress when it suited her.

She pressed dead daisy petals between Japanese rice paper sealed with masking tape and sent them in the mail to her then-boyfriend Jacob, despite the fact that they had recently moved in together. Jacob and Morgan were like those popular kids in elementary school you'd only dream of being friends with. When I would visit them in their loft apartment they'd be smoking an excessive amount of weed and doing things like making electro-pop music and experimenting with self-portraiture. They recorded sounds and conversations and wore homemade clothing. They drank endless shots of Jägermeister at the Bar Biftek on St. Laurent, and by two in the morning they'd be singing Disney tunes while Morgan did her best Little Mermaid impression.

"You better not put that lighter away because I'm gonna need it in a second," was the first thing she ever said to me, following me down the stairs of the visual arts building during a mid-class break.

As we shivered outside together, she lit her Belmont Mild with an odd sort of severity, and as the smoke weaved and wafted around her face she introduced herself with only vague interest.

"Morgan," she said, shoving forward a mittened hand.

"Hannah," I replied.

"I was late for class because I was having sex," she said.

And that was Morgan. Fabulously inappropriate.

By the end of that first lecture she had written her phone number down for me on the back of an ATM receipt that showed her bank balance to be $3.27, and when I got home that evening I ran my finger over the loop of her childishly scrawled "M" over and over again.

When Finn came into my life in September and I introduced him to Morgan it was immediately apparent via all his good breeding that he thought she was inappropriate, and I hid my jealousy and adoration of her behind a pint glass when we would all go for a beer together.

She still calls me her best friend, but everyone was Morgan's best friend and everyone knew that they were disposable. I came to understand that she always had her eye on whatever was better, that pink vintage suitcase of hers perched on her wardrobe like a symbol that she was never too far from taking off.

"I'll send you air mail from Europe, honey. *Air mail.*"

The final photograph I have of Morgan in my meticulously dated collection was taken at the loft apartment on St. Paul, the one she moved into with Jacob and kicked him out of less than five months later when she met *the filmmaker.* (She said the two events were completely unrelated.) I never forgave her for that mistake, a mistake that she wore like a badge, proof that she could do anything she wanted, whenever she wanted, that she had complete control. While she had that badge, I was the one who went to Jacob's new apartment and helped him burn the flower petals pressed in rice paper in an empty coffee can on his balcony, feeling almost as abandoned as he did. She began to disappear from my social map as soon as *the filmmaker* wandered her way.

Morgan vanished so completely that I found myself picking up the pieces of her rampage, returning her messages, making her apologies.

In that final photograph, Morgan is, as always, drunk and smiling, eyes closed, slumped in an armchair that she upholstered herself. Blue jeans, wife beater, pack of Belmont Milds; you can tell just by looking at her that she doesn't give a fuck about you, that she is the kind of girl who would return the clothes she borrowed from you with burn holes in them.

That photo was taken the last time I saw Morgan before I went out west. It's the most accurate photo I have taped to the wall of my overpriced West End apartment, a wall of photographs that is supposed to give visitors that I don't have the impression that my life was once rich and full.

Chapter 05

MORGAN

Often when one cannot retrieve the correct bit of information, some other wrong item intrudes into one's thoughts.

THE MAPLE LEAF MOTEL has scratchy sheets and amorous neighbours at full volume. It is located roadside just across the border between Quebec and Ontario where the signs suddenly become English and you are therefore relieved of the Anglophone guilt associated with spending two years in Montreal without learning enough French to order drinks or direct cab drivers. It's called the Maple Leaf Motel out of some cross border anti-separatist patriotism, the lobby decorated in the worst kind of Canadian iconography, the kind that involves water fowl taxidermy, hockey sticks and red plaid flannel.

At the Maple Leaf Motel the weight of the telephone receiver becomes the clichéd weight of the entire world. Everything is in shades of grey and beige.

And I remember:

The first time I was hit.

The last time I was dragged across the floor by my hair.
The first time he called me ugly.

The last time he told me no one would ever love me.

All those times I remember and these scratchy sheets and the weight of the telephone receiver and the weight of my heart beating in my rib cage, surrounded by the flesh I starved and shaped. I want to disappear into a world of truck stop motels and the late June rain, scrawling love letters on the smudged windows of the Maple Leaf Motel.

Here, finally alone, I try to analyze my obsession with abuse. What is it that wills me to be so wounded? Is it a sad offshoot of a fucked-up youth? A youth where I was trapped in a car, fucked and left for dead? Why is it that I desire the loop of his belt around my neck? That I surrender my flesh to him to be so consumed, so bruised, so beautifully destroyed?

(Daddy's dirty girl. Fucking dirty whore.)

I imagine my real mother in one of these motel rooms, drinking cheap domestic beer in a too-small bath towel. I imagine her brushing her damp hair, pulling on her dirty clothes and meeting a stranger in the lobby. I imagine that she wanted to fuck him and never know his name to prove that she could, and I imagine she did, and fourteen days later she was late. And now I am in a motel room off the highway, listening to Frankie Valli tunes on the AM radio, eating Cheetos and drinking Diet Cokes from the vending machine in the fluorescent-lit hallway. All these motel hallways decorated exactly the same way, with little care and no love, just shades of literal beige and metaphoric grey.

Nothing is ever concrete or defined; everything is simply temporary.

Here I am, in a resting place for the weary, and I wonder how many girls that someone hit or called ugly paced these hallways, drinking Diet Cokes and being twelve, thirteen, fourteen days late. Counting quarters and getting ice and dialling phone numbers because there was nothing else, nothing left to do but wait.

I read the want ads in the free paper of whatever Ontario town I'm in at the Maple Leaf Motel and wonder about the lives of typists and machine operators and telemarketers. I imagine I am looking to rent a one-bedroom plus den or searching for a Lincoln Continental, and my fingertips become newsprint grey like the room, and my mouth is dry and all the imagining of another, better life makes me so tired that I lie back on the scratchy sheets and clutch my stomach that refuses to cramp and a body that refuses to bleed.

Twelve, thirteen, fourteen days late.

People who volunteer on help hotlines always wish you good luck when they terminate the call with you. But it was bad luck that made you call in the first place, and the good they wish you seems almost laughable when you are surrounded by Kleenex and have just spent your afternoon talking to a volunteer counsellor about how you fucked up your life.

"*Bonne chance.*"

At three a.m., CBC television plays an animated version of *O Canada* that they have been playing for as long as I

31

can remember, a watercolour homage to national unity to end the viewing day. At three a.m. at the Maple Leaf Motel I remember the first time someone told me that I would do for now, as long as I opened my legs and didn't open my mouth. The first time a man covered my face with his palm when he came and I knew exactly why he did it. The first time I asked someone to hit me and they looked at me like I was crazy. The last time I asked someone to hit me and they looked at me like I was beautiful. I remember wanting someone to make love to me sweet and slow but being fucked instead, being called a whore because I asked for it but realized too late I didn't want it. Because I never really knew what I wanted anyway.

(Daddy's dirty girl. Fucking dirty whore.)

At the Maple Leaf Motel the sun comes up and I have nowhere to be and nowhere to go but back across the border between Ontario and Quebec where the signs suddenly become French and everything becomes fictional again.

I light a joint and read the complimentary bible in the otherwise empty bedside table drawer, and I notice that someone who has slept in these scratchy sheets before me has underlined certain passages with a pencil. I wonder to myself if the Virgin Mary was pleased when she was told she would be nothing more than a vessel. I wonder if she wandered highway motel hallways and considered that she would be remembered for her purity and her chastity, glorified only for the beautiful burden she carried. I wonder if she celebrated her duty, this burning beneath her skin that

32

would later die for our sins. I wonder if she drank Diet Cokes and searched the want ads for a Lincoln Continental and silenced the voice of her stolen youth and perceived it as her own cross to bear before the cross was even iconic.

I wonder whose faulty memory told the story of her New Testament life and if, in the true script, she wore the crown of thorns.

Chapter 06

HANNAH

WHEN SECOND SEMESTER ENDED that year, Morgan and I made the mutual decision to spend an entire summer of lazy unemployed and briefly employed days on St. Paul in the Old Port of Montreal. She and everyone else lived there like it was some twisted, drunken version of Sesame Street, cashing cheques from Mom and Dad and perfecting a meaningful pose. Even Finn had his own place above the dépanneur before the two of us moved to Vancouver together.

(They didn't move there together.)

The Port was defined by its low rent, cobblestone streets and a steady stream of American tourists taking countless Instamatic photos of Morgan and me on her fire escape as we drank La Fin du Monde six packs and very cheap white zinfandel from the bottle. We'd wave and smile mockingly and visitors from Alabama or Vermont would think we were so French, not knowing we were nothing more than two kids from Toronto who managed to escape suburbia, faking our sophistication with cheap education and good architecture.

Together, Morgan and I would discuss our impending fame and write the scripts of our A&E biographies. We were entirely convinced that our summer on her fire escape would become a page in an art history textbook, a fascinating period and locale of po-mo, alt-rock, Can-con pop culture that teenagers would later try to emulate until they managed to find their own identities.

By then Jacob was only a few weeks gone, unceremoniously removed from the apartment and her life. As a result, the empty loft became a space for complete self-absorption and wasted hours, activities I was happy to involve myself in between waitressing and obligatory summer school courses. Morgan was busy shopping for a roommate to pick up Jacob's half of the rent, busy clearing out the office space to make room for a new body. In the meantime, I was asked to fill in the void, help her lift boxes and destroy the evidence that Jacob ever existed. I was instructed not to mention his name, although that proved difficult as it was one of the few topics of conversation that passed between us during those days on their, now her, fire escape.

That summer, the summer before I met Finn, Morgan got pregnant with someone's baby. During the first week of June, the first week the sun had decided to show its full face and everyone had pulled themselves from hibernation and stripped off all their layers, she told me on the fire escape that she was eleven days late as she passed me a half drained bottle of seven-dollar pink wine. She informed me that it was Jacob's, a product of what she called "a final mercy fuck" before he packed his things, but I was never entirely sure that story held up. Nevertheless, I began spending nights there as well as days, eating pints of ice cream, chain-smoking and listening to a stolen collection of her mother's Motown records.

During the month of June, her pregnancy was not to be mentioned when she drank straight vodka or redecorated the loft by moving furniture around. I made the mistake once of telling her that she shouldn't lift a heavy oak desk in her "condition" and received a death glare and twenty minutes of silence as a result.

Occasionally she made jokes about throwing herself down the stairs or getting me to kick her in the stomach, horrible jokes that sickened me, but that I understood, coming from a girl who believed all emotions were a fatal waste of time. Outwardly the "situation" was a mere blip on the radar screen of her fashionable parties and constant intoxication.

Two weeks after she told me her news she cramped and bled, and I immediately took a cab over to her apartment at three in the morning after picking up chocolate chunk brownie explosion ice cream, some maxi pads and a pack of smokes for her from the Couche-Tard.

She cried and then she laughed and put on some Led Zeppelin and passed out.

That night I slept beside her in her bed, clinging to her like I was a new mother who couldn't stand to be parted from her child for even a moment. Despite her hardened exterior, I wanted so badly to believe she was fragile and wounded, that she needed me to hold her and kiss her forehead while she slept. I wanted to believe that she had felt something, because that would mean maybe she felt something for me.

The next morning Morgan cancelled a previously scheduled clinic appointment. Instead, she went out and bought an overpriced pair of black patent leather kitten heels to wear to a "very trendy" multimedia show. She told me she was going with *Mr. Templeton*, the older man I had yet to meet. She never once referred to him as anything other than Mr. Templeton, as if her relationship with him was the sort where it was not appropriate for her to use his first name.

Morgan left me alone most of the day and night in her recently Jacob-free apartment. Before she trotted off into yet another night, she stood in the doorway of her bedroom and changed in front of me, slipping out of her jeans and white t-shirt into a shiny black dress she shoplifted earlier that day from a department store on St. Catherine Street.

She lingered there a moment, beautiful black hair freshly curled, body sheathed in her sheer black bra and underwear ensemble, basking in both my amazement and disgust.

"Hannah, everyone is going to be there," she said.

Without awaiting my response she slid gracefully into her shiny new heels and applied black eyeliner in the hallway mirror.

I realized then, while watching her paint her pale white face, that I was in love with her in the way that little girls fall in love with their school friends. She stood, semi-clad, in shoes she couldn't afford, slipped on a dress she had stolen, and it was suddenly apparent that the world was incapable of ever wounding her. I was in love with her because I wanted to *be her.* I wanted to be as careless and impenetrable as she was, but instead I ached and yearned and cried over a thousand nothings.

Everyone was going to be there.

For Morgan, that fact was always the reason to go. She was right, everyone was there, and the noise from all their bilingual, trilingual chatter made it easy to forget that life and the world were caving in like her insides. That one day there would be a moment where the pain she wasn't feeling now would punch her in the face and fault her for everything she forgot. All she did was stuff the maxi pads I bought her into her purse and dash out the door, while I lay in a crumpled heap on the floor.

"Kisses. Help yourself to whatever," and she was gone.

Chapter 07

MORGAN

However, several case studies and many experiments show that memories – even when held with confidence – can be quite erroneous.

I WATCHED AS ESTELLA lifted her soup bowl of a coffee mug to her lips, the metallic bracelets on her angular wrists making singsong noises as she stained the white of her cup with cherry pink lip gloss. In a single seamless gesture she wiped away the milk foam that accumulated in the left corner of her mouth and pushed back a stray lock of hair, continuing to tell me yet another story that she was at the centre of. She paused only for a drag of a menthol or to apply more lip gloss and never for any recognition on my part. She had a heart-shaped face with grey-blue, wide-set eyes and an almost unnaturally plump bottom lip. Her hair was blonde and what I imagined people meant when they referred to something as *flaxen*.

The thing I both liked and loathed about Estella on that first meeting was that she had a grace I would never achieve. Her voice was quiet and melodic, but her presence in a room spoke volumes. It was evident that she transfixed everyone on the patio and she just continued talking, unmoved by their attentions.

I noticed a smattering of pencil thin scars on the inside of her left arm as she lifted her mug a second time, and as soon as she saw my gaze rest on them, she yanked the sleeve of her dress over the tiny pink lines without wavering from her narrative.

Estella's mother had died when she was just eight years old, severed to pieces by the metal shards of her red convertible when a middle-aged construction worker with no children made the grievous error in judgement that his mail-order Russian bride would prefer him pretending to be sober and bringing their pick-up truck home, rather than abandoning it at the bar and arriving completely drunk in a cab. After her mother was buried and her father became a drunk, Estella went to live with her wealthy Yorkville grandmother on her mother's side and the household's six Afghan hounds. By age ten she had her first lesbian experience with a neighbourhood tomboy named Chrissie, who invited her over one Sunday afternoon to go swimming in her Wonder Woman bathing suit and "learn how to kiss boys." By age thirteen she had been felt up and fingered behind the Dominion by Steve, her seventeen-year-old pockmarked gymnastics instructor.

The death of Estella's mother propelled her into a very different world of private Catholic schools, cucumber and tuna fish sandwiches made by revolving housekeepers, and all-girl experimental trysts in her pink princess canopy bed. An only child, Estella was an after school special stereotype, blessed with an eating disorder and a dead mother to excuse all her bad deeds.

She didn't see her dad much anymore, mostly because he had remarried and was living in suburbia with an Avon saleswoman in orange lipstick and her four ungrateful and overweight children from a previous teenage marriage. Estella's dad would make direct deposits into her bank account after she moved to Montreal at eighteen, and she would carefully reserve the totals for frivolity; specifically, drugs to share and designer shoes and purses. She told me that she liked the idea of him paying for her to play because he had made everything so difficult to begin with. She despised the fact that despite everyone's knowledge of her father's infidelity and her parents' pending divorce, he got to have the starring role as grieving husband and received an all-access pass to drunk and distant. Her grandmother was the only one who seemed to agree and, as a result, Estella was given an all-access pass to disobedience to compensate.

Estella's most perfected look was bored and disinterested, and she was using it now on a male patron who was making small gestures in her direction to his drooling companion. I imagined she was used to all the attention, that she had been getting it from local tomboys and gymnastics instructors most of her life, and the only way to cope was to act thoroughly apathetic to the implications.

I suddenly was sure I wanted her in my life daily, if only

to deflect some of the attention off of me, if only to finally gain some quiet as she became the prettiest girl at the party and all eyes turned to her.

So I asked her to move in with me, and two weeks later, on August first, she did.

Chapter 08

ESTELLA

I MOVED IN WITH Morgan after I happened to call a cell phone number at the bottom of a "Roommate Wanted" poster tacked to the student centre bulletin board. I met her on a St. Laurent café patio on a Wednesday afternoon after class and she was fifteen minutes late. She arrived flustered, wearing a bright green, ill-fitting dress with a torn hem and gold flats, gripping a paper cup of cold coffee in her hand and an unlit cigarette in her mouth. Within ten minutes she invited me to move in. I liked her right away and knew she would stay out of my business. I agreed and never even saw the place.

Morgan told me that she'd kicked her boyfriend out two months ago and she had converted the office space in her Old Port loft into a second bedroom. Privacy would be facilitated by nothing more than an Ikea curtain hung from the ceiling, but I didn't mind. Living alone was starting to make me slightly crazy, starting to make me sleep with strangers with no one to judge my actions. My former bachelor apartment on Peel Street had become the home of a recluse; I would pace the length of the tiny hallway, kicking away debris to the rhythm of a tiny, tinny radio mounted on top of the empty fridge. I had given the place up at the beginning of the month and had been finding daily temporary solutions since, my belongings edited down until they could all fit into a single bag.

My thought was that having Morgan permanently in the next room would at least provide a small amount of restraint when it came to blind-drunk-take-home companions, and it would be nice to have someone around on a Sunday morning to eat toast and jam and discuss the week with.

In August we painted the walls Hollyhock Red and filled the Ikea bookshelves with art books and design magazines. We had faux-sophisticated cocktail parties, watched foreign films and listened to French cabaret music. Wearing white terrycloth bathrobes, we painted our toenails blackcurrant and talked about how we were better than every other person we had ever met. Life became sweeter with Morgan in it because she had this talent for making all of the things that once brought me high anxiety seem completely irrelevant in the face of a Friday night party across town. She would curl my hair with a hot iron, make it shiny with serum and then lend me her best black dress.

All the fear fell off me and I could focus again.

Then one night Hannah and Morgan and I went to a party full of struggling actors with a twelve pack of Stella Artois and I saw Finn.

Finn. Finnegan.

I had often felt like I had never been in love and couldn't have defined the word if asked. The concept of devotion was so foreign to me, and in many ways absurd, but in the moment I saw Finn all suddenly became possible.

From the moment I kissed Finn, I began to notice elderly couples holding hands on the Metro, the smell of the sky and the smiles of strangers. When Finn looked at me, music and light and colour became frantic and formulated just for my enjoyment. My heart hung in the space between us, skipping and throbbing to pop songs on the radio. The kind of songs they play in supermarkets and dentist offices. The kind of songs that simply fade into the background when you are jaded and numb, when you fail to believe in love and longing.

The marker where love begins and all things previous were merely diversions. The sudden blinding clarity induced by his face meant the possibilities were endless. It was as if I had been sleeping and the world had suddenly woken me up.

When I met Finn, I saw the future unfurl like a white flag of surrender.

I knew in that moment at the party that I could love him. It seemed juvenile to think so, naïve to assume love was that spontaneous, but as I watched him speak in his slow, deliberate way, I was sure I could love him with such abandon and I would find the moment to let him know. I would invite him to come inside my tightly built walls, to share coffee with me in the mornings and kiss me to send me off to work.

I saw a thousand opportunities to find love in the smallest moments that I had so wilfully ignored.

He turned his head in my direction and looked at me with an intensity that assured me that my confessions would be embraced.

But the truth was he didn't look at me. He looked past me.

He never looked at me. He looked past me.

He learned Hannah's name instead.

Hannah found her way into Finn's heart that night, and all I could do was watch from the kitchen counter as she touched him, leaned close to his ear to speak all her pointless phrases. As the evening wore on I grew to despise her, her indifference towards my feelings, her inability to see that Finn was meant for me and that she had destroyed the only moment of love I had ever experienced.

I went home that night with the first person who asked me because that was easier than going home to the nothing that had suddenly become my lot. He smelled like Old Spice and his name was Brad, which I thought was a joke until he told me that he was "between things" and I noticed he was wearing Lacoste. Nobody who is "between things" wears Lacoste unless they have been set up by absent parents and set free to roam Montreal like a carnivore. Someone named *Brad*.

(Someone named Estella.)

He wanted to fuck and I wanted to forget so we pretended to like each other on a futon on the floor in the Plateau apartment he shared with three other equally boring and irrelevant people. When he was done, which was sooner than I had initially hoped, he had the audacity to talk about all his hopes and dreams for the future, which included being employed in sports medicine and acquiring a summer house. And I pretended to sleep, pretended he was Finn, pretended anything so he would shut up.

I was still awake when the sun came up and I snuck down the external staircase, shoes in hand, and headed towards the Metro.

Chapter 09

MONTREAL

In Montreal it's always so quiet in the morning.

She can walk the streets homeward in last night's clothes without fearing that anyone will see her, without anyone wondering where she's coming from and why she's coming home at dawn. The guilty pleasures exist here without the guilt, without the blame that comes when you make your morning escape and are greeted by a thousand morning commuters.

Low rent, sleep too late, out too late last night, can't really remember.

Knowing everyone, connected in some great family tree of debauchery and accidental meetings. Accidents involving an eight-dollar pitcher or two.

She knows there is an angel on the mountain, a monument to Sir George-Étienne Cartier, who watches it all, and that one day soon she will be judged for all she has done. A monument to a father of confederation on a mountain that gave the city its name, a stone angel who watches all the temporary lives of strangers not ready to decide, spending endless hours and dollars on summertime terraces, avoiding so completely the knowledge that this, like everything, will have to end someday: the winter will come like a surprise fist soon enough. In the meantime, she has another drink and says hello to that stranger she can't recall why she recognizes.

People leave here to finally become something, mostly to become successful and unhappy. Mostly to miss the quiet in the morning. The guiltless guilty pleasure. The anonymity of dawn.

And when she goes back again she realizes that it's over. You can't go back to a time where it's quiet in the morning and a blur all night long. You can't go back when all those strangers become people who know exactly what you did last night and who actually care what you did last night. You can't go back, but you always wish that you could.

Winter here is a cold, cruel woman, but every spring she forgets her cruelty and joins the hoards that pile onto terraces and blot out the memory of winter with bière in plastic cups.

Bière in plastic cups to blot out the knowledge that one day this will all end and she will have to account for the mistakes and remember what the cold had once numbed her to. One day, all those recollections will arise with a force to leave her crippled and incapable of forgiveness.

One day, every sound will splinter her into a million pieces, every flicker across a window, every foul mood. A burst of new emotional thrust to choke her, make her cough and splutter, this lonely rolling road where she will watch the warmth of creatures throw themselves together all around her.

But never at her.

Chapter 10

MORGAN

Memory failure – for example, forgetting an important fact – reflects a breakdown in one of the three stages of memory.

HANNAH'S A LIAR.

She's always been a liar.

Despite the art school stint, Hannah's really a writer and, by default, she has no real sense of truth, is consumed by fiction and lives in *Great Expectations*. She wakes up every day to her beautiful made-up life. She exaggerates and assumes and blames me for absolutely everything. Hannah is faultless. In her eyes, my behaviour was unforgivable, when, in reality, it was *necessary*.

Hannah makes up reasons to blame me when, really, she should blame her emotional cripple of a mother or her distant father or her apathetic Finn. Maybe she should lie down on a therapist's couch and work through every hang-up and fear that causes her to lie and blame and cry uncontrollably. Hannah thinks she's got all these problems but really she's just spoiled and self-absorbed. I'm the one who had to deal with the miscarriage. I'm the one who had to run around fixing the leaks in a sinking ship.

Hannah's a writer. She lies. She's self-righteous.

Victim. Victim. Victim.

That's Hannah.

On top of that, she's jealous that I have all these new opportunities and she's out there in cultureless, soaking wet Vancouver with a guy who doesn't love her and never will, sleeping the days away in that tiny, kitschy apartment she can't afford. It's true that I loved her, but I did what I had to do. You can't always think about other people's feelings all the time, anyway.

It all could have been beautiful and it all could have been perfect, but it never is and to believe it will be is idiocy. Perfect would not involve me doing a pregnancy test in the girl's public bathroom on the third floor of the fine arts building.

My severing from Jacob was like painful amputation with the tiniest blades, pain only plane tickets can fix. But I fixed it and I healed it because I had to.

People like Finn and Hannah and Estella have all sorts of opinions on what the true story is, but I can tell you that I came home one day to our Old Port apartment and Jacob was packing his things and, for some reason, that felt good. We said nothing to each other, and I stood in the bedroom and watched him fold his shirts and wrap his plates in newspaper and I breathed a sigh of relief. I was relieved that I never had to ask him to disappear; he just took it upon himself to take down his photographs, divide our CD collection and separate his knives and forks from mine. I had been waiting for something to end just so something could begin and, no matter what anyone said about who I was and what I had done, I felt good that I had been so firm about my need to clear out the passageways of my life so I could finally leave and move on.

By the time Jacob left we had been together for so long it seemed that I had faded into the wallpaper of his every day, another minute detail to go along with his morning coffee and his evening joint.

I met Jacob in high school, had watched him walk around the halls with his guitar case plastered with band stickers, admired him for months before I finally gained the courage to officially meet him on the shingled roof of a house party over a king can of beer. We shared it and a poorly rolled joint in awkward silence and later had awkward sex in the back seat of my parents' wood-panelled station wagon. I immediately fell in love with his slight, angular indie-boy body and the way his hair fell in front of his eyes. The way he always looked away from me when he came, as if he was ashamed of the vulnerability. I would sit in the basement of his parents' house and watch his Tragically Hip rip-off band practice bad love songs about bad women, imagining that one day we would run away from suburbia and all its trappings, get in that station wagon and drive the length of the country together. Make love in rainforests on the west coast and in trashy, fish-themed eastern motels. When he told me he was moving to Montreal I knew I had to go with him, but when I finally arrived six months after he did he seemed irritated that I had interrupted his new and very different life.

I felt like I had done so much for him up until that point, uprooting my life in Toronto to be by his side, pulling away from all the people I cared about and felt safe around. Hannah acts as if I don't understand how she feels about being with Finn in Vancouver, as if she is so beyond me in age and maturity, but I have seen it and been there before, doting on a man you are invisible to, an obstacle in an otherwise exciting life. When I arrived in Montreal it was Jacob's city, not mine, and I always felt like a guest in his life, staring at pictures of various women that hung on his wall and not being allowed to say a word about it. We never discussed the contents of the six months we were apart, but I was sure the women he had framed and hung on his bedroom wall had filled that gap with drugstore perfume and first year sexual experimentation.

I've heard that Hannah and Jacob now send each other postcards about real friendship and love and faith and devotion and loyalty, postcards that they tape to their closet doors and their fridges, satisfied with their own moral superiority.

Fuck them.

The truth is, one by one, the tiny figurines I had placed so precisely in my life were chipped away. Meanwhile, I was having panic attacks in my empty, quiet, Jacobless apartment. All the pages in my personal history had suddenly been ripped out. All the kisses on the sly and fucking in the backseat of a station wagon were scratched out with the pen I had bought for myself.

After Jacob left, I survived with sedatives I stole from my mother and stockpiled when I went home to visit. I medicated and flipped through scrapbooks and watched the same videos over and over again and called Jacob just to hang up, and I lay down in the middle of my empty apartment and felt as alive and as lost as I had ever been. I would submerge myself beneath the oily bathwater of my clawfoot tub and blow bubbles and feel the quiet of it all, lie still and see how long I could tolerate the lack of breath.

I found someone new to fill the creeping void. An older and inviting man who recently left his wife, or who had been left by his wife, making him primed to buy me martinis on occasional Thursday nights.

He adored me. Told me I was intriguing, that my skin was alabaster and I was his renaissance. We drank dark, thick ounces from shot glasses that I later slipped, empty, into my purse, and I danced by myself in darkened bars while he watched me through the heaving crowd.

It was what I needed. I needed to be taken care of. He called me a little girl, and I liked being a little girl. Maybe because of the way my life played out I never got to be someone's baby. My mother was always sick and I was always taking care of everything, and, as a result, I liked having somewhere to go where I was small and perfect, curled into his palm like a child, a pet, a possession valued beyond all others. At least for the moment.

Daddy's dirty girl.

And he told me he thought about fucking me every twelve minutes (even though I knew there were probably eleven women for the other eleven minutes) and he lied and he told me that he loved me and that he would marry me in a heartbeat.

Fucking dirty whore.

As time went on I drank far too many free martinis and dialled six digits of Jacob's new number, and then I called my new temporary old man rebound boyfriend and, under his advice, bought a plane ticket to France with the last bit of credit I had left.

(He bought the ticket. But she can't reveal vulnerability. Can't reveal dependency.)

The only thing left to do now was run, and I decided to run to the most expensive and distant locale I could afford.

(He could afford.)

I packed only strapless dresses, blocking out my rear-view mirror as I escaped down one of my passageways in a new pair of kitten heels.

So now I am reformulating my definitions, trimming the fat, deciding what being in love and being "together" means to me. I have discovered slowly that my definitions are by no means traditional, no dreams of weddings and babies and little pink houses and hosting dinner parties on immaculate dinette sets. My definitions are my own and I am growing proud of them, the prior pathways with their "we're getting married" and "we just bought a house" becoming faulty, so far from the high school girl who fucked in the back of a station wagon, drank Orange Crush and watched a bad band practice while dreaming of road trips that would never happen. Instead, I think of lovers pooling creativity and making love and art and each other better.

They all assume I am cold and hardened, but the reality is that the love is seeping out of me, too much of it to be trapped and tamed and made to cook dinners and fulfill obligations. In those final days when Jacob and I avoided each other and rarely spoke, I likened myself to a wild animal that he wanted to domesticate, afraid that if I escaped I would maul the townsfolk, so instead I was kept inside, instead I would get high and watch TV and quietly rot, cleaning the stove and doing his laundry. No energy in my life, no art, simply a complex structure of baked goods and joints rolled just for Jacob.

Human beings have this innate and punishing need to recount all the beautiful moments that were yesterday, the need to kiss photographs of people long gone and keep their postcards under our pillows in the hope that they will return to us someday.

The past is like so many stones in our pockets as we venture into the sea, causing us to catch in a whirlpool rather than catching the wave to shore.

Chapter 11

MR. TEMPLETON

I TRY TO PRETEND there are other women but there are no other women. There is only Morgan.

She lounges on my four-poster bed in the morning after we have made love for the second time and I have loosened the ties from her wrists. Dressed only in white knee socks and white cotton underwear, she lies on her stomach and stares into her empty coffee cup like a petulant child while quoting the kinds of novels that only people attempting to prove they know something quote. I survey the bruises I have left on her with both shame and pride, watch as she slowly, playfully outlines them with a newly painted crimson fingernail.

Freshly flourishing scarlet palm prints and bite marks, her knees littered with little blue-black kisses from the hardwood floor. Sometimes she outlines them with a ball-point pen, commenting on how they collectively look like tiny countries floating in the sea of her skin.

I know each one acts as a marker to prevent her from

looking elsewhere. As long as she remains transfixed on them she will stay.

She has to stay. Morgan has rescued me from monotony and she has no idea she has done so. I prefer it that way, her lack of knowledge protecting me, at least temporarily, from the power she holds over me, a power that is infinite and that she is completely oblivious to. She is so beautifully nonchalant that way. Everything is a game to her. There is no talk of the future or worries of commitment. No *expectations*. She is spontaneous and ethereal, dancing in night-clubs and singing show tunes in the shower. Sometimes I sit on the floor outside the bathroom and press my ear to the door to hear her sing them, reminding me that because of her I am so far from death, despite the fact that I have reached an age when it haunts me daily.

I have this horrible feeling that it will end as quickly as it began, that she will leave me and the void will return, but for now I am happy to run my fingers over her bleached white curves. I am happy to cook her meals and take her dancing, happy to entertain her with countless visitors and dinner parties. I have no misconceptions about why she clings to me, and as I dole out plane tickets and carry her bags I can only thank fate for flinging her at me so suddenly. The knowledge that one day she will leave me has to be shelved in order for me to be able to make love to her with the perceived veracity she appreciates. It all has to be shelved or I cannot come inside her with the frantic desperation that she longs for.

Morgan first appeared, sullen and argumentative, in the

very back row of one of my film as art overview summer school classes. Despite the immoral abuse of power associated with me inviting her to my apartment after a night class, I could not deny that she was more than willing. It was not something I had ever done before, but I had always been married before, so seeing her there led to me plotting it for weeks, how I would manage to ask her in a way that her rejection would not make me feel perverse and unprofessional.

"My pleasure, Mr. Templeton," was how she replied.

Coy.

More than twenty years between us, but she came back to my apartment after that night class. When she arrived she wandered aimlessly through rooms, absent-mindedly pulled books from their shelves and flipped through them, asking me why there was no furniture, asking me why it had taken me so long to invite her over, and never really waiting for an answer.

I uncorked the most expensive wine I could find and as the bottle was emptied and the candles burned down she was more than willing, and my perversity suddenly became something to be appreciated rather than appalled at. I made love to her that first night on the hardwood floor of my empty living room, the furniture all gone because my wife had taken it from me. When my wife left me with nothing I had no will to argue, and I had never had the strength to replace any of it. Photographs of her remained in their frames because I hadn't had the courage to remove them and finalize the fact that she was gone.

As the floor bruised my knees and I pushed my fractured self inside Morgan, I suddenly became so completely lost, a bright flash of burning white filling my view as I fell face first into miles and miles of unblemished flesh that contorted and curled itself with limitless enthusiasm.

Fuelled by the expensive bottle of red, she asked me without hesitation to tie her up, the only option a gauzy green scarf that I had taken as a token to remember my wife by, now hanging ominously from a wire coat hanger in the hall closet. Morgan asked me to abuse her with words and wrap my reluctant fingers around her smooth white neck, and without argument I obliged, so afraid she would be disappointed in me, so afraid she would walk out the door and never return. She was speaking another language, words my wife never knew existed, and I recalled the times my wife had lain motionless and vacant beneath me as I shamefully finished.

It disturbed me how quickly I could play the part Morgan required, how otherworldly it all seemed to abuse this creature that I couldn't even believe lay beneath me.

I gave her everything she wanted because she was the only thing that appeared that year that made me feel even vaguely alive.

My unbearable dinner companions. My unbearable ex-wife. My unbearable everything.

Until Morgan arched her back and moaned above me, I was convinced I was dying in my pointless degrees and books and boredom, and as her over-dyed jet black hair fell across my white pillow and her red lipstick smeared across her left cheek, I knew that I was validated.

(The minor detail that the lipstick was burgundy and not red, irrelevant.)

"Marry me, Morgan," I foolishly said that first night.

She smiled a wicked grin and said nothing, letting me know she knew very well that she had hooked me.

There is so little I know about Morgan, so little she shows or tells me. I know that she goes down to her local bar at a quarter to nine almost daily. And everyone is there and to her everyone is just as ugly and irrelevant as ever. I know that she has secrets she will never tell because that's the kind of girl she is, a girl with secrets. And I know that she decrees today that life is simply taking and not giving. And I know she asks me, "Does the body rule the mind or does the mind rule the body?"

But she only asks me because she stole the question from a pop song on the radio.

As our time together progressed, we went dancing and drinking at those local bars I obviously didn't belong in, and she would flirt shamelessly with patrons only to return to me and kiss me quickly to the disapproving stares of self-important university students.

When she was offered a joint by a group of slacker intellectual boys on the walk up St. Laurent back to my apartment, the largest, loudest one of them said, "But don't bring your Dad, okay?"

She is careless, but that carelessness got her into my bed in the first place, so I wasn't about to complain as she danced to eighties Britpop tunes and downed countless cape cods in celebration of some random Thursday night. In all her clumsy drunkenness she has an elegance about her that I know one day will come to glorious fruition, and I pray to myself that I will be around to see that day.

Morgan talks to strangers and always accepts the drinks they send over. Unlike the men she was used to, I never express any jealousy, my violence reserved only for her pleasure, and I just watch stoically as they take any opportunity to touch her.

Her shoulder. The small of her back. Her face. Anywhere they can manage.

She thinks I tolerate this because I am mature and she tells me so often.

The reality is I am afraid.

The day I went to court to settle with my wife, Morgan sat in the back row in overdramatic black sunglasses, smiling softly the whole time and twirling her purple gum around her finger as she read a fashion magazine. There they were in the same room – my wife who had taken everything, even a bag of salt and both frying pans, and my Morgan. Morgan and I never once locked eyes in the courtroom, participating in yet another one of her fantasies by pretending we had never met until we returned separately to my apartment and ripped the clothes from each other's bodies in a frantic, animal way that made me forget that I had ever been married and that I had lost everything.

She talked endlessly about how she wanted to run away from it all, would pose like a pin-up girl in next to nothing on my four-poster bed and flip through *Vanity Fair* while nonchalantly complaining of a general feeling of emptiness.

Ennui, she called it, as if she had just learned the word and was trying it on, using it often as a statement of knowledge.

She wanted to drink sangria on St. Laurent patios at every available moment. When we occasionally ran into an acquaintance of hers she would always introduce me as *Mr. Templeton, a filmmaker.*

She begged me to take her on trips to film festivals and speaking engagements, and I gladly took her along, noting that the disapproving stares were only among the university set and that she possessed a charm that penetrated the scholarly and often shallow companions I surrounded myself with in a circle of intellectual elitism. Her laugh was enough to disarm even the thickest of scholastic pretension, and she had my friends lapping up her juvenile speeches with an intensity that was generally reserved for diatribes on auteurist cinema.

Morgan was a sexualized child, and I was not blind to the fact that she was my Lolita, snapping her gum and pulling at her dress, her irresistible naïve qualities in competition only with her blatant sensuality. The sex that coated Morgan was the kind that only comes from the enthusiasm of someone so inexperienced, a kind of raw energy and insatiable hunger that my circle of scholars and I had lost a long time ago.

She had had (or, as I was forced to admit, perhaps currently had) some boyfriend who ignored her, a fact that failed to surprise me. Twenty-something-year-old men ignore the gifts they've been given because they always think something better will arrive at any time but, sadly, it won't, and as I brushed the dust and regret off of me with her irresistible skin, I knew that it could never get any better than this.

Nothing better than Morgan will ever arrive, so she can have all the shoes and strapless dresses and dinners and flights to Paris and San Francisco she desires. It is a small price to pay and I pay it gladly, even on my limited salary.

Despite this generosity, I know she toys with me daily, her laughter piercing and the inaccessibility of her body unforgiving. She will disappear for days and never tell me where she has gone, and I am forced to make love to her with such severity in the hope that my name will be burned inside her so the others will read the ownership like Braille. I find marks on her body, bruises and bites, and I play back the moments we have spent together and I know that another man has planted them there. I count them like inventory and when there are too many I will count them again to be sure, trace them with my fingertips and yet say nothing, constantly afraid that a single word will cause her to walk out the door a final time.

She will leave me.

She will leave me because she has wanderlust. She threatens to run away to foreign shores with no warning. I want to tie her up with my wife's scarf and trap her in my apartment, never allowing her to leave me, pin and mount her like a rare butterfly, but like all the other gifts I give her I also give her limitless freedom at great cost to my own comfort. I am afraid that if I don't put her on a long leash, she'll simply gnaw at my trappings and run away.

Despite all her secrets, there are harsh truths I learned from Morgan that would have made anyone else desert even the smallest connection with her. I learned these truths because there were times when I saw through her, small moments when she would reveal something other than façade to me and I saw that she wanted only to be loved. And when the twenty-something boys taught her she couldn't be loved she sought to destroy everything that was beautiful in the world, all the people who were beautiful in the world, because she hated so relentlessly her own emptiness. Hated the knowledge that she was unlovable, that she was nothing more than a good time to be had in secret moments.

And she was forced to tell me that the reality of her womb choked her into the reality of consequence because I could see it all over her, pale and bloodshot, suddenly disinterested in the lust she always begged for. Part of her wanted someone to hold her so tightly that the hurting would stop, that love would blot out the years of pain and the images of abuse.

Someone to blot out the moment that the hurting began, and that love would bleed into every bad memory until they were all obliterated.

Someone, I hoped, like me.

I held her so tightly to me, only to have her wake the next morning as if it, and I, were a dream she wanted to forget.

"My pleasure, Mr. Templeton."

Coy.

This is the truth I learned from Morgan, the truth she told over and over again: We are all animals. We tell lies because we are hungry and want only to eat.

Chapter 12

JACOB

Curiosity got the better of me on a Friday afternoon and I followed him from the staff lounge, out of the visual arts building and onto the Metro. I did it not because I wanted to confront him but because I wanted to study the way he walked (slow and deliberate), what he picked up on his way home (milk, eggs and a copy of *Harper's*) and where he lived (in a red brick walk-up in the Plateau). I suppose I thought that somewhere between Guy-Concordia Metro and the tree-lined side streets of the Plateau I would figure out why Morgan wanted him instead of me, why she left me for him, but I didn't, and as I watched him methodically search the back of the refrigerator at the Couche-Tard for the latest date his milk could expire, I imagined that he was as insecure about her leaving as I was.

Because, reassuringly, I knew she would leave him, just as she left me and just as she would leave everyone eventually.

The only thing a girl like Morgan knew how to do was leave.

Chapter 13

MORGAN

Details from separate experiences weave together, so that the individual remembering thinks of them as having happened together.

WHEN I LET ALL my shiny little fish swim away from the net I had snared them in I didn't suffer from the knowledge they would never swim back, I simply put my slinkiest dresses into a suitcase and went forward into new nothings and potential everythings.

I am not, by any means, perfect, but Jacob's palms were damp and his brow furrowed, and I was so tired of the arguing and the fixing that I stopped hearing his voice. I only truly left him the day I got on that plane, as he was in my mind until that moment. I got on that plane and there was nothing waiting for me when I got off it. I was standing in an empty waiting area and everything was possible and nothing was probable. I was merely a visitor again, the time clock ticking out as it always did, always would. There was no longer a love waiting for me, if there ever was a love waiting for me.

I am nothing more than an observer.

I envision Hannah in Vancouver, rummaging through the few boxes she shipped west, bogged down by all of her mistakes to the point where she fails to see the Pacific Ocean at the end of her street. She's a fool, forgetting to forge anything new in the fear that she will lose everything old.

There are millions of people and options and days and nights and choices and ideas and mistakes and successes. The phone will ring and not ring and your mailbox may or may not fill with letters of love and hate, but to wait for them is a grave error. Instead, I dream of freighters and steamships and hotel rooms in technicolor locales.

I cut open my net and let all the beautiful little fish swim away into the darkness and I end up floating to a place somewhere on the continent, a place where flash-bulbs burst into shards of fame and gloss; my heels press into plush red carpet and my eyes are blinded by the sun climbing into dying darkness.

And no one can blame me for loving the loss so much.

The whir of wheels kissing runway, face pressed to glass and problems only plane tickets can fix.

I know what they all think of me. Of him. But it has nothing to do with infidelity or opportunity. With free airline tickets or immaculate dinner parties.

I think he is actually healing me.

This aging, blue-eyed academic is straightening me out, shifting me into the scary dark places and forcing me through them. It sounds so cliché, but I can see things so much more clearly when I am beneath him, as if the world has suddenly cracked open and there is so much light.

I am no longer numb, no longer empty. I am feeling something again.

He pushes me to be fearless. His palms press into my flesh nightly, treating me with the same kind of caution that one treats a wild tiger or a broken sparrow. I am both in his eyes.

I will never tell him, but he owns every inch of me and can and will do what he wants with my body. The submission makes me feel so infinitely powerful because one must have power to relinquish it. I leave my body because I care nothing for its curves and angles anymore, and I ask him to care for them for me. He ties it up and leaves marks that validate that it is still alive and not merely a shell to house my disappointment.

In here we can have everything we ever wanted. We can have a third and we can lick and taste some foreign flesh. We can devour other people in a way that is ego-laced and debauched. While he ties me up and ties me to pieces, he will watch me eat another with the same ferocity that he reserves for my flesh. I will fuck myself with the same domination that I reserve for him. My rope burns will be kisses that scar. He can do and say what he pleases and order me to order another to do and say as I please.

I can keep him outside of me. Keep all my stories to myself until I become a beautiful character in a twice-read book. I can avoid being real, paint everything just so that he believes the façade that is me. He can never know me because everything about me becomes ugly once it is known. There were ugly moments in my past when the clumsy boys gave me bruises I didn't ask for. A victim in a tragedy that has been written for years. The stories of starving and rape and bruises that were hidden with pancake make-up. The stories of hating every curve enough to carve them up, cut and mark and hide beneath a cover of lip gloss smiles. I want to receive things asked for rather than be surprised by a sudden fist. I am falling for him. I am falling into him and through every door he opens for me.

Now I am free to consent and free to ask, knowing that he will gladly give me fragments of pain like tokens of tenderness. Like violent violet flowers that will flame and fade from the hidden places on my skin. He will give me bruises like he will make me peppermint tea and fly me to foreign locales.

He abuses me with such tenderness.

(The last time I asked someone to hit me and they looked at me like I was beautiful.)

I will no longer despise who I am for what it is I desire.

He haunts me. I lie in bed at night and think of him. Touch myself and think of him until the room explodes in a shower of colour and light and I lie back glowing, feeling sick with guilt and dosed ill with honey, satisfied completely with how well I have disturbed myself.

"My pleasure, Mr. Templeton."

Chapter 14

I HAVE SPENT MY entire life making the safe decision. I admit that now. I grew up in a small community in Montreal and I never left. I used the same toothpaste and shampoo, ate the same foods, dated the same kind of women. Safe women – girls who dreamed of marriage and believed in loyalty. It was easier that way because it meant nothing was unsure, my path laid out carefully so that there were never any surprises.

Hannah was a complete surprise.

I met Hannah at a party in the Old Port on a Saturday night and recognized her immediately from the neighbourhood. She used to sit outside the dépanneur that I lived above on St. Paul, sipping Coke in a glass bottle from a straw, reading magazines and discussing Foucault and indie rock with the minimum wage punk with the faux hawk who worked there.

She'd steal red liquorice from the counter and chain smoke Belmont Milds on the bench outside, occasionally giving her spare change to the local crazy homeless guy who slept in the Square-Victoria Metro.

He called her the "angel with iron wings."

"Have you seen my iron angel today?" he'd ask me.

Montreal was the kind of place where you could fall in and out of love by the time you'd finished a pitcher and the sun had retreated. Everything was so immediate, and I had always attributed that to the climate, the way the warmer seasons flickered in and out so frantically that the only thing to do was hurl yourself at another person and hope for the best. Montreal was the kind of place where someone always knew (or slept with) someone who knew (or slept with) someone, so it was inevitable that my drug dealer would introduce me to the red-headed, green-eyed girl who smiled at me whenever I went to pick up a pack of Benson and Hedges and a six pack of Boréale.

She was pretty but the kind of pretty that came from endearing quirkiness and not genetics. Tall and slim and always smiling, she was bent on saving the world one schizophrenic homeless guy at a time, and her affection for all things down-trodden was the trait that made you both love and loathe her naïveté. She was constantly rescuing flea-ridden alley cats and writing angry, socially-conscious letters to the editor.

Maybe when I met Hannah through my drug dealer at that actor's party at the end of the summer, I shouldn't have gotten involved with her, knowing what I knew about my situation. I had interviewed for a job in Vancouver and was set to leave in a few months, hiding boxes and packing tape when she came over for a glass of wine or two on a Friday night.

Maybe I shouldn't have let things evolve the way they did, knowing what I knew about her. I had been warned multiple times of her melodramatics, that she was the walking wounded. I had watched her sing and swear and drink wine from the bottle on Morgan's fire escape.

Maybe I shouldn't have gotten involved with Hannah, knowing what I knew about Morgan, knowing what I had done with Morgan. Knowing what I had done to Morgan.

I just couldn't help myself. So when Hannah and her miniskirt sat down next to me at yet another pretentious end-of-summer party in the Old Port, I pretended for a moment that I had no plans to leave town by the time winter hit the city with its annual violent kick. In fact, I think in that blurry, beer-soaked moment I even convinced myself that I had no plans at all beyond that evening. I just couldn't stop. She was magnetic because she was so *unsafe*, the way she smelled like lavender and fit this new theme I had suddenly thrown myself into. I pretended for a while that her constant reapplication of lip gloss and inane stories about her limited life experience was enough for me to stay. Her stories were so full of vigour I couldn't help becoming involved, if only in the way that someone watches the carnage after a car accident with unrelenting interest.

I wrote my phone number down and that was that.

My mother warned me about dating girls like Hannah. She told me they were all baggage and little else, looking for a saviour-type to rope into some illusion of commitment.

Hannah became a trial in so many ways. She had this nasty little habit of keeping all her ex-boyfriends lined up like ducks in a neat little row, each one eager to join the parade of people she signed up for drinks on her few empty calendar days. Her saving the world ideologies also featured a need to save the wounded hearts of men she'd slept with, and I'd have to gently inform her that dinner dates with ex-fucks were not appropriate female behaviour. Ex-fucks like Patrick.

Patrick was the worst of all of Hannah's ducks in a row. He was the boy who came before me, but when I'd bring him up she'd quickly change the subject. They were "just friends" she'd tell me, but I knew better. With his smug look and his fistful of cash, I could read in his face all of the things she had let him do to her body, things that she would never let me do. When I looked into his face, I could see dinners paid for, martinis consumed and him between her thighs.

It seemed that, other than Morgan and Estella, Hannah had no female friends, and I got the impression that her relationship with Morgan was less than platonic anyway. Morgan, in the brief time I knew her, told me that she thought, "Girls should touch more," and "Open relationships are the solution to the fallacy of commitment." Hannah told me that all of Morgan's outrageous theories were right. I did the math on that one but was often too afraid to mention it, just in case the conflict that arose managed to reveal that one forgettable drunk night I had a lapse in judgement and Morgan ended up in my bed.

(The first time a man covered my face with his palm when he came and I knew exactly why he did it. The first time I asked someone to hit me and they looked at me like I was crazy.)

Morgan's presence in Hannah's life brought me high anxiety. The fact that Morgan had broken up with her boyfriend of four years and shacked up with a man twenty years her senior was a dead giveaway that the girl had no morals. She publicly claimed that the break-up and the old man were completely unrelated, but I was on St. Paul that day in the spring and I saw Jacob standing with a pile of moving boxes outside of the apartment he and Morgan once shared, and I knew from the look on his face that her PR campaign was a load of bullshit.

Hannah defended Morgan's actions to the end, a fact that made moving her as far away from the dramatics as possible not an entirely bad idea. It wasn't that I wanted Hannah to be lonely; I just wanted her to have a chance to be the person she should have been.

We were together for only a month when I told her I was moving to the west coast, was poised to leave in December, and, to her credit, she was really supportive of the idea. I had no intention of bringing her with me to Vancouver but she got the idea in her head as a good one and that was that. When I questioned it she would stomp her feet and clench her fists, and I'd smile with all the sympathy I could manage, stroking her hair and pouring her another glass of wine to induce sleep and silence.

One night when we were fucking she blurted out the

words I love you and I was paralysed by the moment, knowing that she was coming with me, chasing me down. When we were finished she lay next to me smoking a cigarette and let me know that she would follow me to Vancouver when she finished her degree in the spring.

I always made the safe decision and in light of my unsafe decision to leave Montreal Hannah made complete sense, despite the fact that I knew one day I would return to what was safe and it was only a matter of time before that safety would fail to include her.

I was well-meaning, but well-meaning is a phrase only used when things don't exactly work out.

It was as if Hannah came from some foreign planet of morality, and she'd always shoot me a violent look of disgust if I even questioned her numerous antics. I learned to keep my mouth shut, perfecting my "interested look" to be used when all her soap opera tidbits and lengthy rants secretly appalled me.

There was a part of me that really did want to give her the opportunity to grow up, to be with me and become a better person. A part of me that knew that she had so much potential to become a calmer, more tolerable, version of herself. That was the part of me that finally let her come with me to the west coast. My influence on her meant she would dress better, speak better, act better. I knew that I was the only person who could do that for her and, despite my aversion to the pressure, I knew that she looked to me to be saved.

Chapter 15

MORGAN

One of the most controversial issues in the study of memory is the true accuracy of recollections.

WHEN HANNAH MET FINN.

We weren't even going to go to that party in early September, knowing it would be full of obnoxious student actors and boring throw-in-the-towel late twenties types with careers and condos and a vague interest in temporarily seducing the naïve early-twenties set to which we held membership. As always, Estella demanded it, equipped with a see-through shirt that did a nice job of letting everyone know her left nipple was pierced. Predictably, Jacob was there and I watched as he ended up flirting with some blonde supermodel wannabe in a fedora for most of the night while her jock boyfriend puked for hours in the only bathroom. All I could do not to vomit myself was watch Hannah's eagerness as she gratefully planted her hand on Finn's right knee.

"He's looking for a lapdog. A *relationship*," I informed

her when she got up to get another cape cod from the kitchen.

"I've been talking to him for a grand total of seven minutes. How could you possibly know that?" she asked.

(The first time a man covered my face with his palm when he came and I knew exactly why he did it.)

Hannah was obviously conscious of the fact that Finn's eyes were on her as she rocked her hips back and forth against the kitchen counter in her belt of a miniskirt.

"His shoes. Comfortable orthopaedic shoes. Watch out Hannah, he's gonna try to put you in his pocket."

What I didn't know then was that all Hannah wanted to do was climb right into some boy's pocket. As much as she would never admit it, she wanted to make steak dinners and give back rubs and fall asleep and wake up to the same face every day.

I just wanted to drive on the highway until the world disappeared from view and what was on the radio was the only concern I had.

Eventually, with all her self-righteousness, Hannah did the unthinkable, uprooted her life for a man, drawn to the smell of sex in unwashed sheets and the need to watch him pour her an early-morning coffee as she sat on the counter in her underwear, transfixed in puffy-eyed admiration. As much as she fought to conceal it with carefully constructed academic ideologies, Hannah's desires included waking up beside a man every day and cooking a three-egg breakfast before he had the chance to stir. Hannah's ideologies became broken plates, cemented back together and painted just right to portray an external domestic calm. As a result, Finn got a pretty, faithful, green-eyed, copper-haired girlfriend and Hannah got a long string of consistent Friday night dates where dinner was paid for and sex was guaranteed.

I admit I was jealous of Finn's predictable stability, so much so that I left Hannah and the blonde and Jacob and Estella and wandered aimlessly around the Old Port's cobblestone streets until the sun peaked its accusing head over the Jacques-Cartier Pier and told me to go to bed. When I came home I found that Estella had handed over her keys to Hannah and, as a result, she was asleep on my couch, Finn's phone number snug between her fingers like a little invitation to escape.

Chapter 16

SHE CANNOT EVEN BEGIN to count the confines within this cloud-bursting cityscape. She fears the rain.

Countless dirty faces and palms cupped for change, so many cups on the walk to the Downtown Eastside, a walk to the office job she despises, a job where she begs for change to save puppies, long conversations on the phone with old ladies in small western towns like Vernon and Prince George.

She becomes blind to both the mountain views and the sleeping bag in the street, looks past and steps over, prays to pay bills and comes home to her asylum, her apartment, to find a notice to end a residential tenancy. The landlord apologizes, likes her, says it's policy.

She likes small spaces, desk drawers and cupboards, cigar boxes and shelves. Compartments. All her belongings fit into four large boxes that she can ship back and forth depending on who loves her, wants to take her with them. On Granville Island she sits in a tiny park with a false pond and watches the Canada Geese and the blue bottle flies that fester as a result, watches the sudden sunshine reflect in puddles as if it is reminding her that it will become rain again soon enough. An all-consuming shade of grey within days.

It's so quiet here. People sleep early and wake early and yet always seem too tired to speak. A coffee obsessed culture that never wakes up.

She is sleeping through the days because she cannot wake to see that this, like the rest of it, will all end soon enough.

Chapter 17

POSTCARD

Hannah,
Arrived in Malaga from Madrid this morning.
After a few hours at the beach I'm off to take the boat to
Morocco.
Be Good.

Chapter 18

HANNAH

FINN IS A PILLAR of strength. A rock to stand on.

But sometimes he is made of nothing but stone.

"That's a very young thing to do, Hannah," he'll say.

"When I was your age, Hannah," he'll say.

When Finn and I argue, which is more often now, I look at him with so much doubt, realizing how little I know about him and his overwhelming belief that all women, including myself, are cruel and manipulative. I'm sure that his belief comes from an old place, a day when he threw a television at the wall after using *69 to find out where his girlfriend had called from, enraged by infidelity and the possibility of another man touching her. He doesn't talk about it. He explains little and says little and does little. Instead we twist around in the same circular debates that never reach a resolution. In the end, we forget why we argued, and we go to sleep clinging to each other like we're all we have in the world.

"You're not going to wear that out tonight, are you

Hannah?" he'll say.

(When she met Finn she saw the future unfurl like a white flag of surrender. She saw a thousand opportunities to find love in the smallest moments that she had willfully ignored up until then.)

I gave up my fears in the hope that he would shield me in a way I had so often shielded myself. I will admit now that I saw a possibility that my desires could be normal and I could want what other girls wanted.

"You're insensitive. You're immoral," he'll say.

When Finn went west, it was snowing and I was left outside his apartment on St. Paul, smoking a cigarette and holding his abandoned potted plant that I named Sylvia.

(It wasn't actually snowing, but that is far less relevant than the fact that he left. Left her.)

I lost all my reasons for staying on that fire escape in the Old Port with Morgan and I packed and went west. Went to a place where the mountains are capped in white icing sugar and creamy clouds burst with the kind of rain that can't decide to be rain.

Strange glass towers reflecting only each other and looming ominously overhead as I wait for Finn to get home from work. Sitting in the solarium window of his twelfth floor apartment, watching the rain coat the city in decay, always waiting for him to get home from work and always wondering why the hand was played this way and not that way.

I surrendered it all in that airport terminal, staring out through the glass onto the runway and into the future. I gave it all up sitting next to him at that party in the Old Port at the end of the longest, hottest summer I can remember, the summer Morgan got pregnant and the summer she lost the baby and the summer we began the process of losing each other for good.

Eventually Finn replaced the love I had for Morgan. He could never be as beautiful as her but he still fit snugly in the hole she left in me. When I was sitting next to him on that overstuffed couch with my hand planted on his knee, I was cut so completely free from the knots of my past. I ploughed into the furtive future with his phone number in my pocket. I left my ties behind and burned my letters and I boarded a plane.

But Finn is so absent-minded; these sacrifices I have made fall out of his head as quickly as I can slot the reminders in.

(After a stop in Paris I headed down to St. Jean de Luz to spend a few days taking it easy. I leave tonight for Madrid.)

My regrets arise suddenly and then scuttle away; they are triggered by the nostalgic smell of grape bubble gum on a freckled girl, the taste of cinnamon praline coffee, that photograph of Morgan taped haphazardly to my wall. I need to spit out the poison periodically and then continue my unwavering devotion, continue making the bed we sleep and fuck in and continue arranging the apology flowers he buys me in a sad chipped vase.

I left all those memories, all those people I loved, to come here to be with him and he avoids that knowledge because he is terrified of it. He cannot see that I am haunted. He cannot see my sadness and regret and longing and nostalgia because he doesn't want to, even though it consumes us both every day.

(I leave tonight for Madrid.)

I could have had so much more than this. I had so many choices. I always wish he could have known that I had so many choices and I chose him. I am glad I chose him, despite the fact that I keep wondering what the fuck I am doing here.

(Be Good.)

Finn, I promise I'll be good.

Chapter 19

FINN

IT'S ALL IRRELEVANT NOW. Now that she's here with me in Vancouver, always above, around or underneath me. Every spare minute filled with her face. A miserable face, full of regret and remorse and animosity, shadowed with the accusation that she sacrificed her old life for an empty life here with me. There is something so very wrong beneath the surface and we will never discuss it, but I know one day it will break and so will we.

I wish I could be more for her, but I am entirely incapable, more lost in my life than I have ever been, more unsure of tomorrow than she could ever understand. She lies in my bed, sleeping soundly between lemon yellow sheets while I quickly dress for a job I despise. I imagine her green eyes beneath her eyelids and I am sorry.

I will never love her enough, and I am patiently waiting for the day it will be over.

She is young and she is foolish, and I want to hold her miserable face in my incapable hands and kiss her a thousand times and tell her I am sorry for uprooting her, tell her I am sorry that she feels like an accessory to my life.

The summer is here again and we are approaching a year. After a year there is still no us. There will never be an us.

We have become those couples that you pity when you see them out together, loathing each other, tolerating each other just to remain as two. Just to maintain a dinner companion. When we meet for breakfast at a diner on Davie Street and I order my eggs poached and hers are sunny-side up, I am hardly ever there. I am distant and I am drained, and I want to tell her I love her but I say nothing.

I merely smile until she is silenced.

Chapter 20

ESTELLA

WHEN I WAS TWENTY-ONE I was on a February plane from Los Angeles to Montreal and we flew into a storm. As the plane started to shake and twitch and the pilot told his faulty stories of "no reason to be concerned," an overwhelming and undeniable feeling of euphoria flowed over me. As the other passengers panicked and held each other close in a sudden gesture of shallow solidarity, I was liberated from all fear because I suddenly knew that my life was meaningless and no one cared whether I lived or died outside of the realm of my tiny universe.

Instead of this admittedly dark thought bringing me sorrow, it seemed only to make me lighter, and I turned away from an old lady praying into her Chicken Kiev and went back to flipping through the pages of my fashion magazine, turning up the volume on my iPod.

When my plastic dinner tray toppled into the aisle I remember smiling, experiencing a feeling pure and blissful. When the Fasten Seatbelt sign went off and I pressed pause to hear the pilot announce we would be turning around to land safely in Philadelphia, I was disappointed that I hadn't plummeted to my death in the exact moment that I could have so gleefully accepted it.

I tried to think of that plane crash euphoria as I lay there on the bathroom floor, but Hannah's sudden frantic pounding on the door broke the memory of it, her screaming for me to answer causing me to finally snatch a towel from the rack. Pressing it to my sliced wrist, I stopped the proof that I was still alive from further staining any more of her immaculate surfaces.

Maybe I knew very well that Hannah would come knocking only after a few minutes, her being the kind of girl bent on saving the world, the kind of girl with such high anxiety that she unplugged everything and checked the stove four times before she ever left her apartment.

Her being the kind of girl who had never really felt loss and yet was afraid of losing everything.

Chapter 21

MORGAN

Swiss psychologist Jean Piaget reported a case of memory fabrication from his own past. Piaget had a memory from early childhood of his nurse resisting an attempted kidnapping, with himself as the potential victim.

WINTER CAME TO MONTREAL that year in the same violent, mocking way it always did, but we, as usual, were unprepared. And despite the fact that fall had warned us for a few months, despite the fact that winter came every year with the same sudden ferocious shock, we all acted surprised and frantically retreated back inside, off the fire escapes and front steps of St. Paul and into a series of Friday and Saturday night parties.

On a Saturday in December, Estella and I went to yet another party in the Plateau and, as always, it was bullshit. A vast array of people I never liked anyway talking about their pending weddings, engagement parties, dinner parties, and couples-only retreats into the wilderness. I watched them carefully, likening their technicolor wardrobes and animated gestures to circus performers. I absorbed all of their singsong conversations in disjointed fragments, piecing the elements together into a single incomprehensible, detestable monologue.

A black-haired, buck-toothed waif of a girl in an emerald green dress kept saying how much she hated Piet Mondrian. I lit a cigarette from the silver engraved case that Jacob had given me for my birthday. The girl went on to express her distaste for English landscape painting and, while she did, she proceeded to spill her cocktail all over the white shag living room rug. *Never Mind the Bollocks* was playing too loud, forcing her to shout her painfully bad art student critique, but I imagine she preferred it that way.

"Where is the passion in a Mark Rothko?" the waif asked her far-too-interested-to-actually-be-interested-and-probably-just-wanted-to-fuck-her companion while rubbing the toe of her no longer fashionable Mary Janes over the now wet spot on the shag.

If I had had the energy, I would have told her that club soda would get that out and that Rothko was in the simplicity. I would have told her it was the intense spirituality of minute tonal variation. It was volumes in silences. That if she didn't hurry the shag was going to stain.

That it was seeing the unparalleled beauty of nothingness.

If I had had the energy, I would have told her to stop talking.

By eleven thirty the waif was still ranting on about her innovative approaches to art criticism and my mother decided to call me on my cell phone after she and I had had about sixteen drinks between us, and after asking me about how school was going, she let me know that she had cancer, or at least they said it was cancer, but it was probably nothing, and they had cut it out of her.

That she had cancer. Again. And they were carving more pieces off and out of her until there was nothing left. *Routine*, she called it.

I couldn't hear her over the Sex Pistols, which was now on its second rotation of the night, but I think she told me she was sorry she hadn't told me sooner. Then she told me that she was sorry she was emotional, something about the codeine not sitting well with the bottle of wine she'd been working on all night.

I had spoken to my mother on the phone after she had polished off a bottle of white wine enough times to realize that this was the point in the conversation where she started apologizing. Crying and apologizing. So I got up from the overstuffed couch, excusing myself to people who didn't notice me leave, and I locked myself in the bathroom.

While seated on the green tiled floor, I stared at what must have been the remnants of vomit that lined the inside of the toilet seat. As I did so she was, as predicted, crying and apologizing for being a bad mother, then adding that she wasn't even my mother, as if I didn't already know it and hadn't known it for years, as if she was telling me for the very first time that I had been adopted.

My "hip mother" who had always treated me like her best friend, a fact that seemed incredibly attractive to all of my teenage girlfriends when I was in high school. They would all sit in my kitchen and ask her for sex tips and general boy advice, drinking the beer she had offered them upon their arrival after school. My mother with one breast, a woman who wore headscarves and talked about birth control and listened to old Carole King and Van Morrison records.

I always resented her for that, the way she had adopted me because she was lonely and childless, barren, the way she wanted to go shopping and talk about sex with her rent-a-friend.

"Ever since you were little I've been far too hard on you, Cathy." she said.

She used my real name. *Catherine*.

For as long as I could remember my mother had been suffering from various ailments, some fictional and others very real. Her insides had been riddled with mysterious growths and invasions, busy foreign cells that had to be investigated and carved out by pleasant, smiling doctors. Her uterus was finally taken as a measure to save her life, the salvation leaving her feeling empty. She spoke about it as if it had been stolen from her, as if thieves had come in the night and taken her capacity to breed. There was a general feeling of pointlessness that fell over her as a result of the theft, merely thirty and incapable of birth, and the depression lasted well into my life despite the fact that my purpose was to blot out that malaise.

Now I imagined her and all her swelling scalpel scars, sitting there at the kitchen table in her pale blue nightgown that my father had bought her for Christmas, lighting another long, thin cigarette and sipping her wine from the hideous brown mug I made her in one of my pottery classes.

I knew that tomorrow she would never even remember making this phone call and that I would never mention to her that she did.

My name is not Cathy. It's Morgan.

I sat there on the green tiled bathroom floor and listened to her apologize for being too hard on *Cathy*, for never baking *Cathy* cookies, listened to her say she would before she died of cancer, that she would make it up to me before she died of cancer, and then I listened to her say it was really nothing. My one-breasted mother saying it was nothing, sitting there in her blue nightgown, one-breasted because the smiling doctors had taken that too.

She claimed that there was nothing wrong and she was fine, and then she hung up on me.

Despite the dead air, I continued to hold the phone at my ear, realizing that I hadn't really responded to anything she had said to me, transfixed by the vomit for about ten minutes until someone started pounding on the door. I unlocked it just as a recently acquainted couple pushed their way in. I realized it was the buck-toothed waif and her companion as I stumbled past them and returned to the living room to try to find Estella, to contemplate the general limitations of life and love, and to down another glass of free champagne.

I sat there on the giant blue overstuffed couch,

thoroughly disinterested as always, smoking and drinking and smoking some more, as one dimwitted loser after another decided to chat with me about their own pending or existing greatness and success. The only one that was vaguely interesting ended up making out with some boring plastic beauty on my fur-trimmed tweed coat in the bedroom. I eventually yanked it from beneath their grinding bodies and made a hasty exit into the hallway, realizing almost immediately that I had managed to drink far too much free champagne and had no money to get home to the loft.

Estella was still back at the party with the house keys, but the thought of talking to her was even less appealing than standing in the cold until she managed to get her drunk slut ass back there.

I couldn't bear the idea of saying to her, "Estella, I'm leaving now because my mother has cancer, but it's okay because it's really nothing and I'll see you tomorrow."

She had already managed to lose her shit on me earlier in the evening for something I did three months ago, something I had absolutely no recollection of doing three months ago, something about Finn and her in a bar hallway, incoherent, but that seemed to be the theme of the year with me, and I had this horrible suspicion that tomorrow I wouldn't actually remember leaving the party anyway, nor would I (like my mother) remember that she had picked eleven thirty on a Saturday night as the best time to let me know she had cancer.

Again.

I could no longer tell if the suffocating emptiness I felt every night was a product of the fact that Jacob had left me (because in that moment it was surely *him* who had left *me*), or if I had always felt this incomplete yearning for something more than a thousand linked evenings of cheap champagne and empty conversation. I thought about disappearing more often now, not in any real tangible Estella-style slit your wrists or pill popping way but, instead, in the way where you want to be invisible, to cease to exist so you no longer have to open your mouth and explain everything, excuse everything, tolerate everything.

I had once been sure, in all my childhood absorption of fiction, that there was a fairy tale ending for me somewhere on the subway, in an airport, a train station. These fairy tale endings always seemed to be linked to modes of transit in some way. Plane ticket fix.

I pulled my make-out crumpled coat around me and stepped out of the apartment building into the street, not entirely sure what time it was or where I was planning on retreating to with no house keys, and the only place that came to mind was Jacob's new apartment.

It seemed like the right thing to do in that particular moment.

I wanted to see him but had no real idea of what it was I was planning to say to him when I did. I just knew that I had this gaping void in my stomach, and if I could no longer fill it with free drinks I would instead fill it with familiar sex. I was so entirely numb that I needed to fuck in order to prove that I still existed, have someone claw at me violently to prove I wasn't merely a zombie shell going through the urban motions.

After the ordeal of picking up a pack of Belmonts and a cup of black coffee on credit at a Petro-Canada on St. Laurent, it actually took me an entire hour to get to Jacob's place on foot, and, as I approached, I realized I hadn't taken the time to figure out whether or not he was there or whether or not he was alone. After slowing my pace and considering this notion, I realized that if he was not alone it would in all likelihood be equally satisfying for my purposes.

Seeing him with another woman would fix the numbness.

The lights were off as I approached, and when I rang the buzzer they flickered on in the bedroom.

(Jacob: Hello?

Morgan: Jacob. It's Morgan. My mother has cancer.

Jacob: What?

Morgan: My mother has cancer again.)

The door clicked open and I ascended the stairs quickly, not having any real idea what I was running towards.

I had fucked so many people since Jacob left.

Nameless, faceless people with French accents and American accents who told me they loved me and didn't tell me they loved me. I'd lost count. I felt strangely divorced from it all. I was generally blind drunk when any act of debauchery occurred, generally couldn't remember any particular event, it all simply bled into one blind fuck out of sheer boredom.

I was hoping as the door opened he could perform that act of charity, curing the blind and healing the sick, one more time before I left this low rent, low life town for good.

As the door opened and he looked at me with sheer disbelief, his hair falling in front of his eyes and his familiar slim, angular body gracing the door frame, the following frantic flow of thoughts filled my inner monologue one after another in rapid, agonizing succession:

I will no longer accept that which I do not want or need. I do not know what will happen now and I am not too inclined to care. I will await messages from across the sea. Maybe God has deemed me to be singular. Maybe I am destined to search and search and never find, because that search will leave me hungry and that hunger will allow me to better serve the universe.

Finally, *Tomorrow I will buy a plane ticket and leave all this behind for good.*

Somehow those thoughts made the opening of his front door far easier to bear.

Chapter 22

HANNAH

THE CURSE OF THE wordsmith is that she cannot differentiate between fact and fiction. Therefore, her past is a carefully linked chain of painful lies and her present is nothing more than the sparkle of swept dust.

Chapter 23

JACOB

So let's talk about fair, shall we?

It was May and I was left standing on the St. Paul sidewalk outside of the loft apartment we once shared, my apartment, surrounded by moving boxes, waiting for a friend to pick me up in a van. When I looked up, there was Morgan, barefoot and perched on the fire escape with this grandiose look of scripted remorse on her face for the benefit of the viewing public. Remorse for everything she had done wrong, so sorry for the pain she had caused, and I was so sorry I'd ever met her in the first place.

The girl I loved in high school, the girl who used to pick me up in her parents' station wagon, and we'd go get Slurpees at the 7-Eleven and spike them with Smirnoff as we drove around listening to Led Zeppelin on the stereo. There she was, hair cascading, mouthing the word "Sorry" over and over with trademark red lips.

(The minor detail that the lipstick was burgundy and not red, irrelevant.)

I met her on the roof of a house party in the suburbs. I made love to her in the back of that station wagon, lost my virginity, took her virginity.

(She lost her virginity well before, but that is a minor detail, now irrelevant.)

There were reasons she gave and there were reasons I invented. Finding herself was one of her reasons and another man was one of mine. Other men was one of mine. It didn't really matter what was true and fair or right or wrong because, at the end of it all, I was on the pavement and she was perched on the fire escape, barefoot and apologetic.

After all the silence between us and all our mutual absence, there was nothing left to do but pack my things and move out. I didn't even argue and didn't even wait for her to suggest it. I could tell just by looking at her that she wanted something (someone) else, and in a lot of ways I completely understood why.

So many things I forgot to say and do, and if we're on the topic of fair, maybe it was fair that I was the one stuck with the moving boxes on the sidewalk, and after my friend picked me up in the van I unpacked all those tokens of the past and managed to drag myself to the Cock and Bull to deposit her memory in a pint glass for good. The jukebox there was full of medicine and I poured endless quarters in it, finding vague solace in bad seventies song lyrics. Each night I was there with a different friend of mine, each one telling me to snap out of it and get over it, each one eventually getting tired of buying me pints and tolerating my drunken rants about Morgan's presumed infidelity.

And yes, I know there was no infidelity; I just convinced myself there was because it was easier to hate her that way.

(There was infidelity.)

When I ran out of real friends to buy me drinks I got convenient ones instead, forty-year-old overweight union relics and francophone separatists, men who were going through or had been through divorces with ex-strippers, men who endlessly explained to me the wicked ways of women from behind their blue-collar moustaches. After a while, my makeshift alcoholic friends would raise their glasses to a mantra of "Fuck Morgan."

"Fuck Morgan," my union would say in unison.

The sickness sets in and all of a sudden it doesn't fucking matter how hard I try, I am completely incapable of being logical and strong. I can tell everyone I know about the new rules of never mentioning her name. I can call Hannah on the phone and tell her I don't want to hear that Morgan misses me and wishes me well.

(Jacob: Hello?
Morgan: Jacob. It's Morgan. My mother has cancer.
Jacob: What?
Morgan: My mother has cancer again.)

I can play pretend and get girls' phone numbers, beautiful French girls with speed habits and rich Westmont parents, and I can fuck them and fumble with the remote notion of being "over it," but when I open my front door much too late on a Saturday night and that perfect face wanders back in, and she takes her place in my front hall like she belonged there the whole time, all I can do is hold a glass of whisky in my sweaty palm, pour another for her and pretend I'm not losing control. I mentally add up the various ways I could kill her and that old guy who stole her away with promises of paid-for airfare, but all I really want to do is kiss her, and as I step outside myself and watch her try to explain what she's doing there at four a.m. I realize there's a degree of perverse hilarity in the whole thing.

The sublime running joke that is my life.

I left handwritten messages on the windshield of her car, the car I lost my virginity in, and watched as the splutter of spring rain peeled the ink from the page, ruining as always all the things I had wanted to say.

I see her at Old Port parties and I ignore her, flirt shamelessly with blondes but look past them, listen closely to see if I can hear her voice over the noise of the party. And every time she laughs I assume she's laughing at me. And every time she looks up at me I wonder if she misses me in her bed.

I always wished she would show up, just so I could tell her to go away, but now, as predicted, I beg her to stay.

She suddenly looks so vulnerable now, cold and quiet with the smell of cigarettes and alcohol all over her, and I ponder taking advantage of her here and now just like she had been doing to me all along. I ponder rejecting her and having her and hating her and taking her to the bedroom and fucking her hard and coming deep inside her before she can say a single word.

And as she stands there in my front hall I want to beg

her to come back to me because, really, I promise to pay attention, and I'm sorry about the pregnancy, but if she'd told me instead of Hannah telling me after too many tequila shots, after it was all over, I would have been there with her in a second.

Instead of saying all these things I end up grabbing at her, if only to prove that she is there, that she is real, and I grab at her to take what I can get before she's decided she's made a terrible mistake and is gone again for good.

Because after all is said and done, after all I've done, that's only fair.

Chapter 24

MORGAN

He remembered his nanny pushing him in his carriage when a man came up and tried to kidnap him. He had a detailed memory of the man, of the location, of the scratches that his nanny received when she fended off the villain and, finally, of a police officer coming to the rescue.

I BUTTONED MY SHIRT and myself back up and left Jacob's new St. Henri apartment, stumbling over shoes as I fumbled with the door handle and burst into the stairwell painted the colour of toothpaste.

I will no longer let others dictate where I am. Where I am going.

I think Jacob chased after me as I ran in the wrong direction up Atwater, past the Metro, away from the loft and towards the lights of Westmount, but I sprinted from him, quicker now that the champagne and whisky buzz was gone.

He was calling my name into the city and I heard it as I ran, pounded the concrete with all the strength I had left in me, cold in kitten heels and stockings in December, and the name he called wasn't mine.

The name I had given myself, the name I had invented.

I told Hannah that as an infant I had been found in the lobby of an adoption agency, tucked into an orange crate and swaddled in torn out comic book pages. That my real mother was an addict from a trailer park in Tennessee, raped after her shift by a manager named Bruno in the storage room at the fifties-themed diner she worked at. Told Hannah she went on welfare afterwards and crocheted tea cozies to stay afloat, found the cozies couldn't cut it and ditched me in the lobby.

This carefully knotted rope of lies so tightly constructed that I was bound by it, believed in it, just as I believed in the name I had given myself before I moved to Montreal.

That name is not mine, I thought, slowing my pace and walking into the core of the city, past the strip clubs on St. Catherine and the drunken boys and the homelessness and the lone churches and the cab drivers and the chain smokers in all-night coffee shop windows and the drunks thrown into the street and the neon and the concrete and the dirt.

I looked in the eyes of prostitutes and johns and boys and girls and bums and cops, past the squeegee kids and businessmen, out-with-the-boys men, and the graffiti scrawled on the wall said *Morgan, this name is not yours.*

After Jacob left our loft apartment earlier that summer, it was cell phones constantly ringing and cigarettes bought on Daddy's plastic and petitions and propaganda and countless dirty little clubs with drinks bought by countless dirty little men. It was calling my father for more money and him yelling at me for the credit card bill and finding a cheque from Jacob for who knows what bill in my mailbox, spending it on more dépanneur wine and a pair of black stiletto boots, instead of helping Estella with the rent on our Old Port hole or fighting the threat of having the phone cut off.

Hannah and I would go to various bars and Hannah would convince men to buy us drinks, so good at the theatrics despite the betrayal of her true nature. We'd call her the wordsmith because she had the ability to get us ninety-dollar bottles of champagne and multiple rounds of shots by giving the "intelligent girl" spiel. She was good at conversation and had it down to a science, the way she would hunt married men on vacation, driven by the theory that they had expendable cash and a low interest in taking us home for a night of infidelity. The best thing about her was that her talent for larceny improved with her blood alcohol content, and nights soon extended into mornings and we'd spend the only money we'd spent all night on the cab ride home. Who knew all of her complex feminist ranting translated into a desperate need for two Volvos in the garage and a complete matching dinner set?

Since Jacob had been gone I also had all of these new, *fabulous* friends care of Mr. Templeton. I started spending a lot more time in his apartment, drinking a lot more wine and doing a lot less. As I was forgetting to eat he was making sure I was fed while I met artists and poets and filmmakers, a wannabe fashion designer and a wannabe photographer, countless street kids that Mr. Templeton cooked dinner for and showed books to, books about German Expressionism, boys who stole his silverware and stole looks at me in my black stiletto boots. The cast of characters were all fictional to me, all in a script that suddenly seemed to be lacking all meaning.

I viewed most of the surreal scene from the older man's four-poster bed and from between the pages of *Vanity Fair*.

I've always felt isolated from other people, always isolated myself from other people. I like the quiet and yet I fear it so completely when it creeps over me late at night. I fill it with music and crayon colour and people I don't even like just to avoid its suffocation. Sometimes I would panic, call Hannah, and she would walk to my building at three in the morning, equipped with Belmont Milds and brownie explosion ice cream, and we'd audio tape ourselves talking about everything and nothing, drunk on toxic beverage concoctions that I'd created from my mismatched liquor cabinet.

We'd sit together on my couch and watch a marathon of cartoons and draw countless pictures, taping them to the wall above my bed. We'd pour out letters to the ones we loved, folding the scrawled notes, tying them with red ribbon and sealing them in envelopes never to be sent. Each one was carefully and lovingly stored in a cigar box knotted with twine that I lodged in the fuse box, a powder keg of our mutual confessions that we trusted each other with.

When I thought I was pregnant with Jacob's baby I named it Gabriel and got in my car and drove on the highway for hours, from Montreal across the Ontario border, thinking about driving off the road, thinking about all our recklessness that we found so amusing when we were in the thick of it. It was all so liberating until I held the very human consequences of it inside me like a weight that made me immobile, a weight I decided to name Archangel Gabriel until I felt it cramp and bleed out of me after I drowned it in vodka and disregard.

I drove for most of the night and then checked myself into a half star roadside motel and watched the Christian Television Network, drinking Diet Cokes and dialling random phone numbers on the large beige motel phone just to hear the random voices of countless strangers. I waited until one of them told me it was too late to be calling anyone and then sat down in the filthy bathtub beneath a scalding shower. I sat there for what seemed like an eternity, crying endlessly in silent hysterics so no one outside the door of room 4B would hear me.

When I finally told Hannah about the baby she fell apart, but by the time I told her I was so removed from the situation that she became obviously disgusted with my visible lack of devastation. I told her it was Jacob's, despite being concerned that she would convince me to keep it because it was "made in love," or some bullshit like that.

The truth, the truth I never shared with anyone, was that in the moment I lost that baby I wanted it so desperately, wanted it more than anything I had ever wanted before in my life. Its face was invented and burned in my mind.

(Invented.)

I eventually told Mr. Templeton a few weeks later, spurred by his desperate questions on why our fucking had ceased, and as I did, an overwhelming and fleeting knowledge of incapability fell over me, an incapacity for feeling that has been following me for years. The emptiness filled my mouth with bile and my eyes burned and I crumpled suddenly, so inappropriately, that I fell face first into his chest and heaved with my own personal pointlessness. I turned and vomited onto the bed, as if the tragedy I had been suppressing in the pit of my stomach needed to be expelled, and for the brief time I lay there in his arms I allowed myself to be vulnerable to him. I let him carry me to the bathroom and watched as he ran the water for me, lay motionless in the bathtub as he lathered my hair, my body covered with the fading bruises he had given me, and a silence between us so heavy yet comfortable that it threatened to continue my sudden flush of feeling into morning and beyond.

Everyone always accuses me of being problematic, but when the loss happened I was only thinking about not causing problems for anyone else. I didn't want some blood-soaked pity party in my honour. I didn't want Jacob to love me because he felt some imposed duty to do so. The fact was that I drank and smoked and lifted heavy boxes until the problem took care of itself in the sudden overwhelming heat of a late June night. Hannah managed to keep her mouth shut, and I eventually managed to move on, despite the fact that the hole inside of me increased in size at the thought of all the things I could have had.

Now here I was, in kitten heels, my shirt buttoned quickly and, therefore, wrong, running from Jacob's new apartment months after he had left me, or I had left him, or whatever it was that happened. I was walking aimlessly again in the middle of the night, trying to find out who I was amongst all the fake shards of ceramic and realizing all too quickly that he was not what I was or could ever be, his hands like insects crawling on an exterior that had become an impervious shell.

My hair was a mess and my lipstick smudged but I was happy again.

My life was a piece of smashed ceramic, broken and glued and re-broken and re-glued over and over again.

Chapter 25

HANNAH

I HAVE AN INTENSE affection for all things broken.

While all the girls in third grade ripped the pink clips from each other's hair in the schoolyard because they were all in love with the boy who had that quintessential boy band haircut, I was busy crushing on the small angular one who sat quietly at his desk in the back row. I watched intently as he picked at his sensitive skin, complained about debilitating sinus issues and took medication for an allergy to grass. In my mind, that boy had the depth of an ocean and I am sure he grew up to be sensitive, beautiful and effortlessly stylish.

That sniffling boy with his faded blue tracksuit was my first three-legged dog, and since him other people's cast-offs have populated my life, broken befuddled things that others deem useless that I value above all else.

My tiny apartment in Vancouver is a maze of misused relics, each one with so much promise and intended for a reparations project I have not yet had the energy to begin.

Toasters line the kitchen counter like soldiers, wounded and waiting. A worn armchair sits patiently. It holds onto the promise that I will reupholster it, surrendered to me by the lover of an elderly man who died of a heart attack on the eighth floor of my apartment building.

"I never liked that chair anyway," he had said when I retrieved it.

Beautiful and perfectly new things have always been suspect to me. I scowl at city skyscrapers and version 9.8.2's. I prefer that time test the technology so the flaws are no longer hidden behind the shiny exterior of right now, waiting to surprise you with disaster at the most inopportune moment. I trust the predictable failings of ex-boyfriends in bed and a horrible east side office job. I trust the integrity of a can of baked beans or a box of Kraft Dinner. The faithful simplicity of a bottle of cheap blush wine. The charm of vintage cardigans and the smell of second-hand books. The loyalty of things other people cast off when they outgrow them.

I realize there is an error in this ideology.

The error was revealed when I took on feeder mice as pets, ill-bred, frantic creatures destined to end up in the bloated belly of a snake. I bought each one for ninety-nine cents from an overweight, bearded and bitter man at a pet store on the east end of St. Catherine. He took me into the back storage room to a cage where there must have been over a hundred of them crawling all over each other in an immense squirming mass, and I picked out two and named them after eighties female singers.

Cyndi Lauper died the morning after I bought her. Six weeks later Linda Ronstadt lay with her head in a food dish, dead from a stroke.

Uncertainty is my certain enemy, and in my realm of broken toasters sourced from the nearest Value Village, I am comfortable with the knowledge that they are broken and will be until I decide they will be fixed.

I cannot tolerate the unknowns of waiting for something unbroken to break.

And what I wanted Morgan to understand before I left Montreal was that I loved her because she was broken. I wanted to tell her that part of my pain was that I saw myself in her. It was too hard to say that to her without coming across as critical, condescending or didactic. I wanted her to know, when I held her close to me that night she bled that child out of her, that I loved every inch of her and that I would never do to her what came so easily to the men she had loved.

The night she lost that baby she was finally vulnerable and discarded, and I wanted only to love her with the kind of abandon that would never be permitted. Her sudden tragedy only made her so much more beautiful to me, the vulnerability of that moment such a contrast to her hard exterior. I only wanted to love her and kiss her soft alabaster face with the kind of tenderness reserved for children.
I saw myself in her, every juvenile mistake and every jump forward she took.

All she ever did was jump.

So I got on that plane and I went west and I never really

thought about the why of it all. I did it because it was just too easy to do. *Brave.* They all called it brave, which makes me laugh now because it was the most cowardly thing I could have done at the time. Sometimes I think that I went to Vancouver because I was running away from Morgan and not because I was following Finn. The true bravery would have been to stay and kiss Morgan's full mouth and suffer the consequences of that action.

Suffer the humiliation of her inevitable rejection.

Bravery would have been to feed her champagne and after the fifth glass confess, but instead I ran from her like I ran from everyone and everything my entire life. Living in all these fictional moments and telling my compulsive lies because that was far easier than facing reality, far easier than feeling anything. So began my reality of lying beneath a man, waiting for him to finish.

When he would tell me he loved me, I would close my eyes and imagine that it was her voice. Imagine it was her lips that kissed my brow and her fingers that pulled back my hair.

Instead I went westward, as we do into the future, across the prairies into the mountains, until her face was a dream that never came true.

Chapter 26

MORGAN

WHEN MY ADOPTIVE MOTHER was growing up she slept in the same urine-soaked bed as her four brothers and sisters. I don't think about this as I walk down the street from my loft apartment to pick up sushi and kitty litter on Interac at the Hasty Mart.

A six-year-old girl in a pink dress holding a clear plastic bag with a tiny fish swimming in it comes into Nijo Sushi with her mother while I am waiting for my maki to be prepared. She stands in front of me briefly and I think of Gabriel as she holds out the tiny bag towards me, smiling. I take a drink from a $2.99 bottle of pear and pomegranate juice and smile back at her and then return to an outdated fashion magazine with a sticker on it that says, "Magazines are for everyone. Do not take out."

When my mother was six years old her father threw a brick at her because she was too scared to use the outhouse and, instead, shat under the back porch in the dark. She laughed the entire time she told me this story.

I don't think about this on my way back home from Nijo Sushi when I run into the bartender at the St. Laurent venue I frequent on Thursday nights. The conversation is chock full of words like "darling" and "sweetie." His seething vanity shames me as I realize I have decided that pyjamas are the uniform suitable for take-out and kitty litter pick-up.

My mother sits at home all day and watches soap operas and Dr. Phil while chain-smoking Benson and Hedges Slim 100's and drinking cheap white wine. I press decline on my cell phone when she calls because I am too busy with martinis and other forms of urban self-indulgence to care.

The people who live on St. Paul Ouest sit on the front steps and fire escapes of their buildings in terry cloth bathrobes while drinking La Fin du Monde. They talk about politics and indie bands while painting their toenails.

They all own vintage bicycles.

I eat sushi in my pyjamas and I decide the food is mediocre and that I won't order from Nijo again. I then decide the litter box can wait another day. I decide that Estella can deal with it this time, despite the fact that I haven't seen her for days.

My mother has never had sushi, was never able to order it between dodging bricks from her father and avoiding piss in bed, but she buys it for me from the Loblaws in little clear plastic containers when I come home to the Toronto suburbs to visit. She takes it out of the fridge half an hour before she predicts I'll be hungry because she knows I enjoy it room temperature. It is stale and so obviously from the supermarket but I say nothing because she is so proud of herself as she lights another Benson and Hedges Slim 100.

And it occurs to me. No one has ever been proud of her but herself.

She had me to be proud of her, and I wanted a Gabriel of my own to do the same for me.

Chapter 27

However, when Piaget was 15 years old his nanny decided to confess. She had made up the entire kidnapping story to attract sympathy and even scratched herself to make it seem real.

AND SHE CONFESSED TO me over much too strong long island iced teas that she had made it all up.

There was no angel Gabriel tied up in her womb, no blood expelled to mark his passing. She confessed that it was only occasionally that she realized that she had lied, that the love she had formulated for this imaginary child was so intense that the fiction had adhered itself so tightly to her gut; she had actually cramped and buckled when the illusion had miscarried so completely.

She confessed this on a Thursday afternoon at the Bar Biftek between drags off cigarettes and sips of two-for-one drinks. She had invented it because she had wanted it, and she had lost it because she knew the reality was that girls like her can know nothing of want because they can know nothing of having. They simply pull their clothes on haphazardly at dawn beneath the accusing stare of photographs of other women, happier women worthy of framing. Women smiling in bikinis on trips to foreign locales, licking ice cream cones and holding puppies. Women the sleeping men are too afraid to remove from frames because they are the women that validate them as more than mere animals. She would never wind up in a frame, so she invented something growing and living inside her, something fictional to love and fill her, and just as she created it she killed it in her mind.

A last chance to fulfill a want to never be fulfilled.

And she confessed that while they slept she would rifle through their scattered belongings, searching for evidence of things that proved love was a reality that lay outside of fiction. Notes scrawled on notepaper in great looping handwriting, whispering love in the form of grocery and to-do lists. She would hear other women's names on answering machines, names like Annabelle and Bridget, beautiful, chaste names worthy of flowers and vacations and concert tickets. Girls that studied art history and drank light beer. Girls whose fathers bought them shiny red cars and whose grocery baskets contained things like baby spinach and baguettes.

Not the kind of girls who liked to be tied up and called names. Not the kind of girls who would do all those things that were asked of them.

She told me she would wander their apartments while they slept and steal tiny mementos that love existed, snapshots and scrawled notes and receipts, and despite the lie that she participated in nightly when she fucked and felt nothing, she would take these tiny pieces of evidence and paste them into an endless series of scrapbooks. She would flip though pages and believe, unequivocally, that if she rubbed her fingers up against the evidence their messages would bleed into her and she would suddenly become a girl worthy of a picture frame.

She was ready for that day, the day when she could sleep soundly in the snug space between arm and chest. Ready to hear the sound of shallow breath and ready to be adored rather than consumed. Ready for the filth to finally stop, when she could slit open her skin and pull someone inside without fear that they would steal every last thing.

But that day never came, and the illusion that it would was miscarried along with the fictional child embedded inside her flesh.

Chapter 28

HANNAH

THINGS WITH MORGAN STARTED to fall apart quite quickly after Finn left in December, and there was no real way to prevent it. She wasn't really up for propping me up anymore. It's the way life goes I suppose. The way Polaroids fade to yellowed relics of better times and there's no way to preserve or even to remember their technicolor fantasy.

I began to get increasingly sullen and would be prone to spontaneous crying fits in public places: bars and cafés, parties and art openings. No one seemed to want to hand me the box of Kleenex but, instead, began to avoid me and my miserable rants like the plague.

Perhaps we all just outgrew each other, but any random martini-laced night began to feel forced and awkward, as if we all had far too much baggage and too much to do to maintain it anymore. Morgan's beauty, her spontaneity, failed to impress me any longer and she began to develop a very distinct ugliness about her that was directly related to how careless she had become. I couldn't forgive her for all the things she had forced on all of us and as much as I tried to hold on to those last details that kept me close to her, one by one they faded until eventually I no longer received tiny cardboard messages of affection or fame from her anymore.

Where life had once seemed so vibrant, I now felt like I had developed a coldness, a numbness about me and around me that I couldn't shake. Even as I dramatically pounded on the locked bathroom door, trying to save Estella from whatever she had decided to do to herself that week, I was really just going through the motions, doing what was expected of me, not really caring.

When I bought my ticket for the journey to Vancouver I knew that I was sealing my fate as the kind of person who was too exhausted to truly care about the Morgans and Estellas of the world and all the naïve dreams that came along with them. I simply sold my things and gave it all up because that was the only thing left to do, fall flat face first into a bottle and bathe myself in a disconnected way of life, a life where I was paralysed by the fear of recollecting, afraid of remembering the beautiful things that came before the constant rain.

Somehow I actually forgot, was no longer able to piece together events or recall moments, the past fading into a blank page and my life starting again, born in the arrivals gate of the Vancouver airport. I knew I was miserable, but I was almost too miserable to even notice I was miserable. I became locked in a routine that only perpetuated my apathy to change, becoming satisfied with how mechanical things had become.

The hardest thing about leaving was realizing that people are self-absorbed and betray each other everywhere and that the poison was not restricted to the former geographical centre of my universe.

Highways twisted through mountains and the air smelled clean and wet and redwoods dwarfed me and life lay before me, yet I was unable to process the landscape and appreciate how glorious it all really was.

So, instead, I sat in Finn's apartment in an old extra-large Smiths t-shirt and from the twenty-second floor watched the beautiful underage rent boys sell themselves on the corner down below. I felt isolated and listless, and I knew I wasn't in love with him and probably never was or would be but, rather, was merely afraid of the thoughts inside my head, afraid enough that I didn't want to be alone long enough to hear them.

It is easy to hide in a world where mountains tower and rain keeps you inside.

Where your love isn't real and you're too afraid to admit it, too afraid of yourself to listen to the truth, too afraid of life to live it alone.

Chapter 30

MORGAN

WHEN SHE TOLD ME Finn was moving west I knew it would be mere weeks before she decided to follow him like the lap dog she became.

Funny that after that night she met him she never talked about what came before him. Never mentioned that boy who she claimed shattered her into a million tiny shards.

Patrick.

That guy was like a disease, and his name was all over those postcards still lodged in my fuse box.

Chapter 31

POSTCARD

After a few hours at the beach I'm off to take the boat to Morocco.
Be Good.
Love,
Patrick.

Chapter 32

HANNAH

Patrick.

Beautiful, made of good Patrick.

Patrick, somewhere on the continent, a voice far in the back of my skull, swimming there like some strange, forgetful fish, pearled and perfect in the cool recesses of my mind.

Before Finn there was Patrick.

(I am faithful, Finn. I am being good.)

There was slow dancing in the university cafeteria with Patrick and urging Patrick to shoplift from the Dollarama on St. Catherine. There were shots of tequila at the Biftek with Patrick and foreign films at the Cinémathèque with Patrick. There was making love to Patrick. There was loving Patrick.

(Be Good.)

I thought about Patrick while standing in the terminal in Montreal, waiting for my plane to Vancouver. Before I boarded I stared out onto the runway, surveying all the winged metal beasts that lifted off and landed, my face pressed against the cold of the glass. It was the moment I finally severed from Patrick, after years of back and forth bedroom accidents and uncomfortable hung-over morning afters. I felt strangely like a piece of my flesh had been carved out and eaten, my heart devoured by rabid dogs right there in the waiting area of the terminal.

After I met Finn I'd tried to ignore Patrick like some bad memory to blot out, safe from view. All the time I had wasted with Patrick when I could have been thinking and writing and saving the whales and cooking feasts and feeling good about who I was and working on who I could have been.

When I deplaned in Vancouver a boy, barely twenty with shaggy hair and untied shoes, approached me and passed me a torn out and carefully folded piece of notebook paper before he retreated quickly up the ramp to baggage claim. I unfolded it to reveal a carefully drawn pen and ink portrait of me staring out onto the runway in Montreal. He had captured me while he sat five rows in front of me on the plane that crossed the prairies.

I quickly shoved it into my hip pocket as I scanned the welcoming crowd for Finn's face.

Patrick's postcards from various locales filled my mailbox, brief passionless messages scrawled across them as if he was giving me tiny fixes to keep me addicted. He was sleeping on beaches, spending too much money that wasn't his to begin with, his feet filthy because he refused to wear shoes and his body sore from the night before because he refused to say no.

Be Good, those postcards said.

(Finn, I promise I was being good while you were gone.)

I hardly spoke Patrick's name to anyone after I met Finn, despite the fact that I managed to fuck him twice during the first few weeks Finn and I were together. I was like a drunk who needed a couple of gin and tonics before rehab commenced. I decided to go cold turkey and not see him for months on end. Messages were erased and emails deleted. I did it for Finn but he didn't seem to notice and certainly didn't mention it, just like everything else I had done for Finn since.

When Finn finally left for Vancouver I didn't really see any reason to stay away anymore, so in January I rode the Metro to Patrick's one-bedroom apartment in the student ghetto the first time he invited me. I savoured the naïve notion of friendship, although I think I was fooling myself as I carefully dressed in a weather inappropriate pink pin-striped strapless dress.

Be Good, those postcards said.

Patrick was the king of all fence-sitters, graced with big, beautiful blue eyes and the kind of eyelashes that stretched out and flickered, the kind that only children have when they're convincing you they can do no wrong. He had an apathy to life that only those who know their charm and wealth can get them out of any fix could have. During my visits to his huge one bedroom apartment I would scan his face for some reassuring fault, some blemish that would affirm that he was not the angelic treasure I had mythologized him to be. But even his flaws were beautiful and, above all else, it was his immaturity and disregard that people were magnetized to.

Every shirt Patrick owned was meticulously ironed. He hung up his dry cleaned and pressed blue jeans in careful rows in his walk-in closet. He knew how to choose a quality bottle of wine. I was apt to buy the one under ten dollars at the dépanneur. He was the kind of person who would sooner die than embarrass people with his personal problems. The greatest failure to him would be the remote possibility of him imposing any vaguely suicidal or murderous thought he had. I often told him I wouldn't be surprised to find severed limbs in his freezer. Nobody could have been that together without hiding something truly horrific.

I managed to conceal the visits from everyone, even as they began to happen almost daily. I knew I would be criticized, and I knew Finn would explode with jealousy during one of our few sporadic long distance phone calls if he found out. I hid all of our meetings, not that there was anything substantial to hide, making my way over there four or five times a week to watch horror movies and World Cup games, seated one foot away from each other on an eight foot couch. Sometimes I'd arrive after an eight thirty a.m. class and take a nap in his bed while he watched cartoons or cooked me a late breakfast. In all my yearning, we never touched each other, never retreated back to our previous games of lust and mistakes.

(This is a lie, but she believes it to be true, so it fails to matter that it isn't.)

Being there with Patrick brought me a solace and escape that were only really needed because the loss of Finn had left a vacancy waiting to be filled with someone in close proximity.

(This is a lie.)

It was a comfort that I wanted to believe was unblemished by all the past chaos and torment that had fallen between us and our sheets.

Chapter 33

FINN

IT IS TRUE THAT in the end I no longer wanted Hannah, but the idea of anyone else having her was intolerable, and the idea of Patrick having her was enough to breed murderous thoughts.

The one and only time I ever met him, apparently by accident, was at a bar on St. Laurent where Hannah and I had met for an after work drink. When he came in and walked right up to us, I could see him staring at her like he owned her, like a possession that he once bought that now belonged to someone else.

He was so intoxicated that he screamed his greeting at me like I was a competitor for a trophy.

"So you must be Finn," he spat at me, his leg propped up on the chair I was seated in and his face in uncomfortable proximity.

"You must make Hannah *very, very happy*. Hannah's never happy, and look at her now."

As he exploded into laughter, Hannah looked up at him

in a moment of enamoured nervousness and discomfort.

He had had her, touched her, been inside her so many times. His smug face testing and taunting me, seeming to say, *Go on, ask about the last time I had her. Ask me how it was. Ask me when it was. . .*

"Good ol' Finn. You saved our Hannah, didn't you?"

Hannah frowned, but I could tell she was enjoying every moment.

You saved Hannah, didn't you?

That seemed to be everyone's opinion.

Chapter 34

TORONTO

"I MISS YOU, PATRICK. I really do."

Liars and writers. The two are interchangeable.

She was always so demanding. Always in need of so much attention. She'd laugh when she was kissed. She'd line up shots and tell stories, tell secrets, tell lies. She'd scream his name loud enough for the neighbours to hear. She'd cut his back open with her fingernails and fake it every time. The shots lined up were the reason she eventually told him she faked it every time.

"Do you still think about sleeping with me?"

She asked him this question on a night bus on the way to her parents' house in Toronto for a weekend in March. It was their final year at university in Montreal and she had a need to run away for a few days and asked him to run with her. While she waited for him to answer the question she braided her hair into pigtails and then unbraided them again.

He never answered the question.

When they got to Toronto he gave her mother a bouquet of flowers and ate the fish dinner with canned corn that was prepared for him. He watched her sleep from the floor of the bedroom she had slept in during high school.

Of course he thought about sleeping with her. Of course he still thinks about it now. Of course he tried to make love to her one more time before they both left Montreal for good.

(Of course he made love to her one more time.)

"You never *made love* to me, Patrick. You fucked me."

Which was fair.

She's never seen the south of France or taken the boat to Morocco, but there was something about her hungry voice, the way her jealous eye would scan his thumb-tacked map. She used to call him Home because, as she made very clear, she felt like she'd never really had one.

He thought maybe if he asked her at the right time she'd want to be a part of his wanderings, the two of them together on trains and buses and her in a bikini on the beaches she'd never seen before.

He asked her and she chose Finn instead.

Then he lied and told her that everything would work out just fine.

Now he buys drinks for girls with varying accents in varying locales, and he watches them drink their martinis and rum and cokes and he only sees her eyes staring back at him, mocking him with their distaste and indifference.

"I miss you Patrick, I really do. It's just that. . ."

(But, yes, of course he made love to her one more time.)

Chapter 35

POSTCARD

Had a great time in Paris.
Heading back to London tonight.
Wish you were here.
Be Good.
Love,
Patrick

Chapter 36

ESTELLA

You're on the line between fantasy and reality, and you question whether you're alive or dead, and you question your ability to care, and you question your ability to feel anything.

When I was a teenager, my girlfriends and I would climb to the rooftops of Toronto apartment buildings and strip naked in the rain, snapping photographs and kissing each other with smeared lipstick and smudged eyelids, just children in Wellington boots and their mothers' make-up.

When I was a teenager, I fell in love with those glossy heroin chic fashion photographs of fourteen-year-old girls who looked dewy, moist and half-dead, like interchangeable coat hangers to hang million dollar Dior dresses on. I loved the way they looked so anonymous and irrelevant, wasted and post-orgasmic, beautiful in their decay.

I lay down on Hannah's bathroom floor and I felt that feeling of decay wash over me like a tonic that healed every wound in me. Hannah who was packed and ready to fly to see her beloved Finn the following day. Hannah who would leave tomorrow on a vacation to decide whether or not she would leave for good.

It was February and it was cold, and I felt as beautiful and glossy as those layouts. Filmic. Frozen in that final moment, forever naked and young in Wellington boots in the rain.

Now, don't misunderstand. I didn't want to slit my wrists in some melodramatic princess moment. I wanted to do it because I wanted to feel something *other than*, anything at all.

I wanted to make a mess on Hannah's bathroom floor and have her clean it up, have her call Morgan screaming and crying and regretting everything. Have her cancel her ticket to Vancouver and never get the chance to decide at all.

I wanted to do it because she took Finn from me.

Carelessness and selfishness and blood and fantasy and reality and blood, and Morgan and Hannah would never shut the fuck up. They'd just never shut up, their pretty, perfect voices always in my head, lost in a maze of their own self-righteousness, their false sense of entitlement everywhere, all around me.

Hannah stole Finn from me.

I was so tired. So tired all the time.

I slit one wrist the wrong way deliberately in Hannah's bathroom while she was dreaming her dreams of Finn and the move west, celebrating with some sedatives and wine while watching infomercials. I didn't have the courage to slit the other one. I just wanted to go so far, know that what was inside was still warm and flowing because everything else felt so cold. I mostly did it so she would know what she had done to me with all her talk of Finn and Finn's arms and Finn's cock and Finn's paid-for dinner dates. I had a collection of tiny marks on the inside of my thighs and wrists that were evidence I had tried to feel it before, tried to cut into the hard exterior that the world had forced on me.

When the tiny pink badges swelled and healed I would find satisfaction in the scarring, but I never felt that the tiny shallow indications proved anything substantial. I collected them and hid them with long sleeves and bracelets, like secrets lined up waiting to be told.

I wanted to reaffirm my faith in scented notepaper, looped handwriting and the uncompromising reality of scars. I wanted to open all the doors and the windows and throw away the gears and springs. I wanted to be flesh again, tender and pink and marred by all the possible moments that wound, but it was like none of it happened at all, and all that was left were those tiny pink marks that silently suggest that there was once something inside to hold in.

They never listened, and I smiled and smiled until there was no more smiling left to do, and while the party whirled around me I was trapped in a tiny pocket of silence and words and theories, and I wanted it to finally stop.

I wondered at what point I became so hidden, forgot about the kind of person I was, the one who would stuff love notes into a locker and watch, invisible, as the boy I put into poetry read them. I would observe his slow grin, despite the fact that he would later mock the looped hand-writing on scented pages to his friends.

I wondered what happened to the girl who had no fear, the one with scraped knees who turned cartwheels and hung upside down from the tallest trees. The one who watched him read the love notes and knew that a light shot from every slit in her, that she could warm the coldest heart with the weight of her devotion.

I knew something of loss. My mother. My father. And now Finn.

Hannah was the girl who knew nothing of loss yet downed her wine and choked back her sedatives and was doted on like a sickly child, never to blame and never saying thank you. Finn had left her and everyone would put their arms around her and tell her to go to him, to be strong and brave and book a flight. Hannah, the girl who had Finn. Poor, tolerant Finn, who was forced to listen to all her endless speeches. Beautiful, patient Finn, who will have to look at Hannah's miserable face every day.

Finn should have been mine, and I never once mentioned that to Hannah, that I had actually met him through Morgan a week before she had, at a bar on north St. Laurent, and the three of us drank too many cosmopolitans and whiskey sours together, and he pressed me up against the wall in the darkened hallway, next to the women's bath-room, and kissed me with an intensity that made my knees buckle and I had to grab at him to prevent myself from fall-ing to the floor.

I never told Hannah that he pushed one hand up into my shirt, into my bra, and another into my waistband, his fingers finding the places on me that thirsted, screamed, for the kind of pleasure that no one had ever provided. I moaned there in the darkened hallway and he removed his hand from inside my shirt and pressed it over my mouth, his rhythm gaining intensity until I came quickly, suddenly, two of his fingers inside my mouth, lodged between my teeth, the rest sprawled across my face.

(The first time a man covered my face with his palm when I came and I knew exactly why he did it.)

Then he forgot about it and forgot about me and before I could remind him (because he would have remembered) she was all over him at that party in the Port. I knew he was going to be there and I was dressed and ready to remind him, but she cornered and coerced him before I had a chance to open my mouth.

I wish I had had the chance to give Finn everything he deserved. Finn would have loved me in a way that he never could have loved Hannah's grating voice of consistent complaint. It should have been me who sat next to him that night, and it should be me who wakes up next to him every morning in the pale grey light of a wet west coast morning.

I pressed a pink hand towel to the feeble, shallow slice on my wrist, its depth by no means fatal but closer to that line than the tiny scars that surrounded it. Blood on my electric blue dress and blood in the sink and blood on the floor, and Hannah pounding on the door like she gave a shit about saving someone other than herself.

I knew that Hannah would find me on the bathroom floor and I knew she would tell Morgan, and I was glad because I wanted Morgan to feel guilty for always coming down on me, always ignoring me, always implying that I was useless, as if she was everyone's favourite and I was an accessory to her very interesting life. I wanted that feeling of apologetic remorse to pound at the cold black hole where Morgan's heart should have been.

After Finn had made me come in the hallway next to the women's bathroom at a bar on St. Laurent he went to get us another round and I returned to the table.

Morgan looked at me, a filthy grin on her face and her eyes averted.

"I fucked him, you know."

"When?"

"Last month. After me and Jacob broke up."

(The after part is a lie. But she believes it to be true, so it fails to matter that it isn't.)

She fucked him and he had been inside her and she didn't care, because she never cared about anything. She had fucked him and left before daybreak, never knowing that he was perfect and beautiful and mine.

"I fucked him and I can barely remember if it was any good."

(There was infidelity.)

Then she laughed maniacally, slapping the table with her palm as Finn returned with our drinks, and a wave of nausea overcame me that erased the ecstasy from moments before. Finn smiled at me, but I was elsewhere, Morgan still laughing and a sour liquid creeping up from the back of my throat.

"Maybe you should just end it, Estella. Get it over with."

Blood on my dress and blood in the sink and blood on the floor. I opened my purse and groped for pills. Blood on my purse and my stockings and on the floor, and Hannah screaming and crying and pounding away at the door. It was so cold and I felt beautiful and glossy and forever frozen in the final moment, the plane falling out of the sky and a smile spreading across my lips.

Naked and young, kissing girls in Wellington boots in the rain.

"Maybe you should just end it, Estella."

It was all Morgan's fault.

Her voice in my head would never shut up.

Chapter 37

VANCOUVER

You could write about France, but you don't know France.
You know absolutely nothing about France.
Nothing at all.
Only postcards from France.

Chapter 38

HANNAH

The Vancouver Aquarium Marine Science Centre is open 365 days of the year.

The only two otters at the Vancouver Aquarium are lying on their backs in the water, propelling themselves in circles with arms linked like synchronized swimmers, like lovers in those first flashes. They spin gracefully around their tiny pool in their faux Canadian wilderness, and Finn and I watch as we share a too-small cup of vanilla ice cream that tastes like it came from a powdered mix left in a kitchen storage closet for too long. It is October and it seems too cold to be eating over-priced ice cream, but ice cream is the thing that lovers eat, and we are still technically lovers, seated on a park bench and huddled under an umbrella in the rain watching otters spin in circles.

Finn loves me, I am sure of that, but there is something consistently uncomfortable between us, and now that I have finally decided to leave him we've come to the Vancouver Aquarium because it was on a list of things I wanted to do when I moved here. I came here because the first and final thing I wanted to see was the Belugas, but now it is these love-struck spinning otters that are ushering me east, and the entire scene seems so ridiculously melodramatic and filmic that I am tempted to tell him that I was only kidding and rush home to unpack my four large moving boxes.

(All her belongings fit into four large boxes that she can ship back and forth depending on who loves her, wants to take her with them.)

Lately Finn looks more tired than usual, his features puffed up and his hair overgrown in tufts at the base of his neck. I would like very much to attribute this lack of sleep and grooming to my departure, but it is more likely late nights at the office and pending deadlines that have caused him to look out of sorts. Not that I find him any less attractive, in fact, the contrary is true. He has become far more real to me in these final weeks, the way he has let his laundry and dishes accumulate and his waistline spread. In the grey light of yet another rainy Vancouver afternoon he seems to be more the person I would have wanted in the first place, rather than the iconic good boy I wanted so much to want. I admire the strong, angular nature of his features as he licks his pink plastic spoon and then absently lodges it between his teeth.

"We'll see each other at Christmas. You can stay with my parents in Montreal," he says suddenly.

I nod in response but continue to watch the otters, knowing that he has turned in my direction and is surveying the subtext of my expression. By now he has learned that I am a terrible liar, that my face always gives me away, and I assume he is searching for a sign that there will be no Christmas in Outrémont with me, no quiet, muffled sex in the guest bedroom while his parents cook salmon and red onion omelettes together for our breakfast.

The truth is, I can't tell if there will be sex and omelettes because I have given up entirely on wishing for things to pan out in some perfect, picturesque way.

All I have to count on is this moment in October, and I cling to it and his arm in the Vancouver rain.

A city where I now live.

Where the rain became an easy excuse for seclusion and singularity.

The city where I lived.

Chapter 39

FINN

PERHAPS I STAYED WITH her because she was the only one I could stand.

And then I couldn't stand her anymore.

Chapter 40

POSTCARD

Hannah,
I'm back in London and would love to see you sometime.
When you're ready, just let me know.
Be good and take care,
Patrick

Chapter 41

VANCOUVER

WHAT SHE SAID: I left Finn and Vancouver eventually.

What she meant: Why don't you cut the goddamn fucking umbilical chord of your goddamn co-dependant mother, you fucked up oedipal freak who can't sever the ties, can't pay his phone bill, can't remember to pay rent, can't do laundry, but is self-righteous enough to tell me how to live my life? To tell me I am "immoral" or from another planet while you have a fucking chronic drug habit, no friends, can't cook, are completely narcissistic, staring into the mirror so proud of yourself and your expensive clothes, making me feel bad about myself so you can feel better, telling me what to wear and how to dress and what to say and then getting me home and scolding me. And you strung me along for over a year, told me not to have "expectations," while I cooked you dinner and made your bed and cleaned your clothes, and you called me ungrateful?

Ungrateful? Wow, you fucking bought me all this fucking expensive bullshit I didn't need, clothes and shoes, while I couldn't pay my rent, while I WAS STARVING, working a shitty job, hating my life during endless days of rain just so I could live in the same city as you, support you and your goals and your dreams, and you never gave a shit about mine, were more concerned that I was cheating on you when you cheated on me and all I ever did was sit around in my pyjamas and cry my eyes out that I gave up my whole life for you, gave up the only person I ever really loved to be with you.

And you never even knew that, and I wished you could have known that, but would it have mattered? No, because it was all about you and all your fucking needs all the goddamn time, but I was made to feel guilty that I was closing in on you, crowding you, and YOU LIED ABOUT YOUR SEXUAL HISTORY JUST TO FUCK ME WITHOUT A CONDOM ON NOW TELL ME YOU FUCKING BASTARD THAT I AM THE SELFISH ONE AFTER YOU LIED TO ME JUST BECAUSE YOU COULDN'T GET IT UP WITH A CONDOM ON YOU IRRESPONSIBLE ASSHOLE.

Now look at me and tell me that I am the selfish one, when you insisted that you come first every time, that you come every time, when you slept through every time that I was sick, when you wanted sex when I was sick, when you accused me of being a dyke just because you were lousy in bed, didn't care that my sex drive was fucked, and you sucked in bed, sweated all over me and grunted like a fucking pig, and then afterwards would accuse me of cheating on you like it was some weird fetish for you. You sick FUCK. The way you always corrected me, had to prove you were better at something, that you had been there and done that and you were so cool when you were younger, when you were my age, and oh the ladies just fucking loved you and you could dance so well, when really you're just a big fucking loser who wasted his talent in a thankless industry and will always be a lonely sad fuck with no friends because no one really likes your self-righteous attitude anyway.

FUCK YOU.

Chapter 42

HANNAH

I LEFT FINN AND Vancouver eventually. It took me many long days of rain to do so, but one day I came over to his apartment in the middle of the night and gave him my iron.

"Why are you giving this to me?" he asked.

"Because I never use it and it's too heavy for me to ship to Toronto."

And that was that.

It's a horrible day when you wake up and realize that all your successes and failures are made up of someone else.

Finn ignored the fact that I was wrapping my dishes in *The Georgia Straight* and donating my clothes to charity. He ignored my empty apartment, and he ignored the plane ticket in my purse. He ignored it all until the day I took a cab with him to the airport and by then I was already gone.

"Hannah, don't leave me," he said as we drove through Kitsilano.

I braided and unbraided my hair, a nervous habit, saying nothing. Feeling nothing. Deciding I needed a haircut, deciding I needed something better.

"Hannah, don't leave me."

But I left Finn in November, eight months after I arrived, on a 6:45 p.m. flight to Toronto Pearson, and when I got off the plane I fell into my mother, exhausted after trying to make the unworkable work. When I finally unpacked the containers I had shipped across the country, I realized how numb I had been, finding them to be full of pointless items that had plotted to make a hasty escape. Earl Grey tea bags stuffed into a chipped vase, bars of soap slipped into mismatched socks. My life had become a plastic Tupperware container full of photographs and flyers, postcards from places I wish I'd seen. I had nothing to show for the time before and nothing planned for the time ahead.

Finn and I made some sort of vague effort to nurture the slow death of our relationship over the next few months. There was a Christmas in Outrémont and I did visit him in Vancouver because I was jobless and convenience allowed it on his dollar. When we returned from the airport to his apartment we clawed at each other's bodies with a new ferocity, fucked and then collapsed on the couch, spent. Finn lit a joint and we watched Jeopardy together in silence, as if I had never left him, as if I didn't live a life invisible to him in another time zone and climate.

"You could come back, Hannah."

"No I can't, Finn."

It took some time, but I finally realized that Finn treated

me more like an inconvenience than anything else. Retrospect is funny that way. Now, I could make a huge list of all the stupid, ugly things he did to me and everyone else, but when I moved west I was fully transfixed. The boy that was overweight and disturbingly conservative, to me was perfection and beauty and a salvation from a sordid past. It's only now that I can recollect that his teeth were crooked and his credit cards were maxed out.

I wanted it so badly that I wrote it and read it and rewrote it until it was rationalized right. The story was edited to have a happy ending, but, the truth was, I got on a plane and left him, left the blindness behind.

(Or he left me.)

I could remember the colours and the shades of that day we met so clearly, the lemon yellow of my button down shirt and the blue of his eyes and the way he fumbled his words when he spoke. The way he put his hand on my leg in a gesture that promised this time everything would be different, this time I would be someone's.

And while he spoke, while he gave me all the reasons we could never walk forward through all those doors that swung open the day we met, I remembered the last time I saw him through the back window of a cab leaving the circular driveway of his apartment building, remembered how perfect he looked there in the rain that seemed to always fall, and I knew I would never again want to hear his voice or see his face.

In that moment in the rain, blurred by the back window of a Vancouver yellow cab, he was perfect to me, and I couldn't bear ruining that fiction for myself, having it all disintegrate into a nothing of hurtful phrases and hated conversations.

He let me go so I could finally be loved, or at least that was the lie he told, or I told, the lie we all tell ourselves when everything we have invested now seems so meaningless in the face of failure.

All of a sudden, it was like it never happened at all. It was fiction, a book I read, a story I told myself. The same way Morgan was nothing more than a character in a play.
I am afraid of forgetting. I think people fabricate because the fear of forgetting is so huge that it is better to remember a lie than to forget the truth.

Because now I can't remember what he looks or smells like, can't remember how he took his coffee, can't remember whether or not his thinning hair was a figment of my imagination, or a figment of his imagination, or real. Can't remember what shaving cream he used, what life was like when I slept next to him every night. What mornings were like when I woke up next to him.

What life was like with him.

In books and films and operas and plays, lovers are separated by consequence or death or sin or society. They never simply agree upon the impossibility and the impracticality of the situation. They never cease speaking to each other under the premise that the union is irrational.

When I was a little girl, my mother used to comb out my long hair in front of the mirror on her antique dresser, and she would tell me it was important that I found a man who deserved me, one who could truly appreciate how beautiful and perfect I was. I have since changed my perspective on the issue, realizing that I have yet to find someone I can see any beauty in.

Perhaps the issue is not what people see in me but rather what I see in them.

(All her belongings fit into four large boxes that she can ship back and forth depending on who loves her, wants to take her with them.)

When it ended between Finn and me, I wanted to hear the sound of my own voice inside my head where no one was telling me what I should want or love or wear or drink or eat or feel or fuck.

All of them were like that, Finn and Morgan and Jacob and Estella, little snapshots of colourful characters that I could no longer prove were real. A whole wide world that I had made up and left behind in the moment the plane left the runway.

I am waking up from this dream.

Chapter 43

MORGAN

The events Piaget remembered so clearly from his childhood had never actually occurred. As a result, he concluded that the false memory was probably implanted by the nanny's frequent telling of the original story. Over time, the scene became an actual event.

THEY SAY (WHOEVER *THEY* ARE) that remembering is merely a function of chemicals, which is a strange reality considering I spent the majority of my life both combining and avoiding the combination of chemicals that cause me to become hysterical with grief.

Succinct. They (whoever *they* are) always said, "Be succinct. Clarify."

They said, "Let your reader know where you are coming from and where you are going. Let them know where the end is."

Where the end is:

My mother finally died on a rainy Wednesday afternoon in April and I remember feeling it in the form of a nausea that I assumed was food poisoning before I even got the call. It was my father's sister Vivian who did the honours, calling me from a payphone in the hospital, slotting in an endless supply of long distance quarters until I finally reacted.

Because, at first, I didn't react.

"Cathy, did you hear me? Your mother's gone."

The truth was that I had expected it for months. It had been over a year since that phone call at the party. I knew that by then they had hacked enough off of her and out of her that there was nothing left but a tired, pale woman in that same blue nightgown, a woman who had every piece of what made her a woman taken from her until she was left with, and was, nothing at all.

When I hung up the phone I pulled on an oversized black raincoat and a pair of Estella's too-small black Wellington boots that I found in the hall closet. After writing her a brief note in lipstick on the hallway mirror stating I'd be gone for a while I walked slowly down the steps and out of the lobby of my building onto St. Paul and got into the wood-panelled station wagon my mother had permanently lent me because she couldn't drive anymore.

For a moment I wondered if it was my station wagon now.

Once I crossed the provincial border I pulled into the Maple Leaf Motel for a moment to call Mr. Templeton and let him know that my mother had died and that I would be gone for a few weeks. We had been together, in some form or another, for close to two years now and as he offered to come and be with me, to stand by my side at the funeral, I simply replaced the phone on the receiver and thanked the desk attendant as he eyed me sympathetically. I stared at his round face, his nicotine-stained beard and slightly crooked glasses, absently wondering if he recognized me, wondering if he knew that all my roads seemed to end up at his hated place of employment.

That all lives ended and all changes commenced at the Maple Leaf Motel.

And at that motel, in the rain, in Estella's ridiculous too-small Wellington boots, while the desk attendant stared at me, I suddenly realized that I hadn't cried yet. I wouldn't actually cry until a full twelve days later when I dropped a bag of groceries on the suburban tree-lined street I grew up on and bent down to collect the broken eggs and dented cans. A middle-aged man walking his dog would find me there, seated on the curb, and offer to help me with my things, and I would only be able to say, "But you can't help me."

No one can help me.

I was always so horrible to that woman, resented her so completely with all her faults and needs and ailments and desperate pleas for attention, her desperate desire to be loved. Even in death I could only pity her, pity the way people had hurt her for decades and she simply accepted it without remorse. When I occasionally visited and looked at her sick in her bed, a bed that in recent months she never moved from, I realized that no one was ever allowed to hurt me like they had crippled and wounded her, and if they did I would simply dispose of them, force myself to feel nothing.

Because if I allowed it, I would end up like her, broken and skeletal, a wounded, carved up woman served up to death in her Martha Stewart bed linens, eating soft-boiled eggs and counting down the days until the disease took all of her.

I was constantly afraid of becoming her and her bleeding heart, petrified of subscribing to her way of taking everyone into her immense embrace and letting them curl up and steal and suck everything from her while she showered them with affections and apologies for being alive, for being herself.

I got to the house I grew up in six hours later, stumbled onto the dark green paint-peeling front porch in Estella's Wellington boots just as night crossed into morning, and my aunt, her face bloated and smeared with mascara, greeted me at the door. She said nothing, simply fell into me – crying – with an expectation that I would do the same.

I didn't.

I am assuming that the chain of events that led to Jacob and Hannah being at the funeral involved Estella calling Mr. Templeton and Mr. Templeton telling Estella about my whereabouts and then Estella proceeding to inform half the world of my tragedy. Because the following week they arrived at the church, in black with arms linked, their faces apologetic yet strangely or, perhaps appropriately, distant, and I was able to avoid them for the majority of the day, locked in one-sided conversations with distant relatives whose names I did not know, eating pickle spears and dev-illed eggs in my aunt's musty Mississauga rec room.

It was Hannah who approached me first, as it appeared Jacob didn't have the opening line to break the silence that had existed between us since that night more than a year ago that I appeared at his front door. I noted how different Hannah looked as she greeted me with a hug, her hair no longer long and red but now cropped short and sun-kissed, a change I assumed was a result of her year without a real winter on the west coast. She was dressed immaculately and respectfully in black, which immediately made me regret my choice to merely comb my hair and throw on a pair of jeans. I was even wearing Estella's boots, a product of the fact that I hadn't managed to pack anything in my hasty decision to drive directly to Toronto. Despite this absurd-ity, it seemed oddly fitting that I cared so little about my clothing, and the reality was that no one else had seemed to notice anyway.

Hannah and I sat down on my aunt's brown floral print sofa and she took my hand in hers. We sat for a moment in silence.

"I heard you moved back to Toronto," I said, assuming small talk to be the best segue.

"In November. I left Finn," she said absently, squeezing my hand and staring at her shoes. Or maybe at my shoes. Estella's shoes.

"I heard that. I'm sorry it didn't work out."

"Now's not really the time for you to be sorry, Morgan." Fair enough.

I noticed then that she had yet to make eye contact with me since we had been seated and because of that I had a sudden urge to run, since it appeared obvious to me she was prepared to launch into a speech that she had been rehearsing and that I was certainly in no position to hear.

Then she launched.

"Morgan, I miss you. I thought of you the entire time I was there. How things could have been different between us. When Estella told me your mother died I wanted to see you. I needed to tell you the truth. Can we go somewhere private?"

I nodded quickly and she pulled me to my feet. I saw Jacob in the corner of the room, talking to some relative I had never met and watching us leave in a way that suggested he would soon follow. The truth was that I desperately needed to leave, regardless of whether or not I wanted to leave with Hannah. When she escorted me through the tiny kitchen, I snatched a mickey of vodka from the counter and we headed to the back porch. The two of us sat at the top of the three stairs that led into the yard. I unscrewed the cap on the bottle and passed it to her while my aunt's geriatric black Labrador retriever chased imaginary insects through the grass. It was quiet on the porch and I was glad Hannah had rerouted me there, despite the fact that her hand had suddenly crept onto my knee and she was absorbing a second ounce of vodka.

"Hannah, I'm still seeing Mr. Templeton," I felt the need to inform her.

"Almost two years now, I hear."

"Yes."

She passed the vodka bottle back in my direction and for a moment looked like she might say something.

Considering the sudden freedom that my dead mother afforded me, I decided to relish the moment.

"Hannah, I fucked Finn. Before you met him."

"I know. I don't care."

With that declaration her fingers reached for my neck, lingered there for a moment, and as she cupped the back of my head with her palm I remained transfixed as she slowly leaned forward and kissed my mouth.

I remembered the first time someone told me that I would do for now, as long as I opened my legs and didn't open my mouth.

The first time a man covered my face with his palm when he came and I knew exactly why he did it.

The last time a man, or two men, or five men followed me in a car after dark.

The first time I asked someone to hit me and they looked at me like I was crazy.

The last time I asked someone to hit me and they looked at me like I was beautiful.

I remember wanting someone to make love to me sweet and slow but being fucked instead, being called a whore because I asked for it but realized too late I didn't want it.

Because I never really knew what I wanted anyway.

Hannah's breath was hot and her vodka-soaked tongue tasted clean and numbing, and in an effort to vacate from the dull grey of loss and a parade of nameless relatives I bit into her bottom lip and pulled her towards me, pressing myself forward and groping to find my way into, under, the hem of her knee-length black dress. She smelled like lavender and returned the gesture by clumsily reaching into the neckline of my shirt and then into my bra, her breath quickening suddenly, panting out four quiet words as the dog chased the sparkle of swept dust that flickered in the warm light of evening.

(Her present is nothing more than the sparkle of swept dust.)

"I love you, Morgan."

She did or she didn't, but it didn't matter. It just mattered that there was *other* in the moment, a feeling tangible and large enough for reality to hide behind, large enough to absorb the fact that my mother was in the ground and I hadn't cried, and wouldn't cry for another seven days.

And on the top step of my Aunt Vivian's back porch my fingers had found their way into her underwear by the time the porch door swung open.

But I was careless and numb and tired and hadn't cried yet.

I simply continued my search inside her, my search for something else in the hot, damp folds of her flesh, while Jacob looked on.

Chapter 44

MR.TEMPLETON

THERE IS ONLY MORGAN.

That summer when we first met we went to the park together. We lay sprawled out on a blanket in the sun, and as she leaned in towards me her breath was hot and her vodka-soaked tongue tasted clean and numbing, and in an effort to vacate from the dull grey of loss I bit into her bottom lip and pulled her towards me, pressing myself forward and groping to find my way under the hem of her knee-length black dress. She returned the gesture by clumsily reaching between my legs, then into my jeans, her breath quickening suddenly, panting out quiet words as an ownerless dog chased the sparkle of dust that flickered in the warm light of evening in Lafontaine Park.

(Her present is nothing more than the sparkle of swept dust.)

"I love you, professor."

And she did or she didn't, but it didn't matter. It just mattered that there was *other* in the moment, a feeling tangible and large enough for reality to hide behind, large enough to absorb the fact that my wife was gone and I hadn't cried, and wouldn't cry for another seven days.

And in the freshly cut grass of Lafontaine Park we finished a flask of vodka and my fingers found their way into her underwear.

But I was careless and numb and tired and hadn't cried yet.

And I simply continued my search inside her, my search for something else in the hot, damp folds of her flesh, while strangers walking dogs and eating ice cream looked on.

Chapter 45

JACOB

WHEN I WALKED ONTO that porch and saw Hannah and Morgan together I should have felt anger or jealousy or disbelief, but I felt only relief.

Because, reassuringly, I knew she would leave her, just as she left me and just as she would leave everyone eventually.

Leave me, and him, and Hannah, and everyone.

The only thing a girl like Morgan knew how to do was leave.

Chapter 46

MORGAN

AND YOU CAN WRITE about France because you know France.

Now that I am robotically designed, steel and springs and gears, no one coming or going has the force to cripple me, and I feel nothing.

So, instead, I have Saint-Tropez on a Sunday with strangers, sipping champagne from the bottle, my feet caked with sand and my lips fresh and raw from too many, so many, kisses. Conversations with foreign cab drivers and chances taken, money rapidly dwindling from my left pocket as I walk barefoot with a pink vintage suitcase containing a broken hairdryer. Down to my last pair of clean underwear in a café where the waitress has one eyebrow, refills my coffee, lost in some strange town, further and farther away from home.

I send postcards from tiny countries with foreign languages and landscapes.

We all have a secret life, a life quiet in all its volumes,

a life that very well does not truly exist because we will it so. We carve it deeply into our hearts, so deeply that the muscle crawls and folds over it, tightens like a knot around it, until its very motion is the beat itself.

The whir of wheels kissing runway, face pressed to glass and problems only plane tickets can fix.

Chapter 47

TORONTO

Everyone is posing again.

Standing around like painted dolls and talking in code, lust and mouths and spines exposed in the glory that is a midnight empty glass moment, billiard balls crashing together and bodies waiting for last call to crash together.

We've got time. We've got so much goddamn time before we die.

That's what the exposed flesh says nightly, the code, the language that states we have so much time before we fade, so let's get broken now before we can no longer fix, no longer heal, over the coffee and newspaper of yet another empty Sunday afternoon.

She told me she liked to go to a local dive of a bar just off Yonge Street near Bloor and fill the jukebox with quarters that should have been reserved for laundry, sprawling her long limbed frame and famous faded red hair across its surface as the blue collar men stared gratuitously at the line of white between her jeans and her too small t-shirt. An exhibition of those small, smooth, allowable spaces. Tiny pieces that peek out and send greetings from hemlines and waistbands.

With a beer bottle with a torn-off label in hand she forgot about how numb she'd been feeling for what felt like forever, how she felt as if she was sleeping through life in the cold grey of another grimy Toronto February.

She told me she should get more sleep, more time, more moments of bliss, more lives without fear or consequence or failure. He had inhaled all of her time and she had forgotten how it all worked, and now she was sleeping through moments, forgetting the past the way one forgets a mediocre film.

She told me she knew she was waiting but she didn't know what for. Perhaps someone beautiful to erase the ugly inside her, destroy it so completely that she was no longer the walking wounded, no longer so crooked and broken and singular by way of her lack of belonging. She told me she despised this brand new need to leave, fuelled by the constant gamble between waking up lonely and colliding with something larger than herself, something that had an equal capacity for pain and for pleasure.

No one can break things if you don't let them borrow them, she said as she tipped her glass back and stared past me, empty.

She told me she wanted only wildness, was so bored with the lacklustre. That in the numb of another February she had decided to no longer fight, that she would no longer beg and plead for a love that would never come. She would let it come naturally like the seasons do, a dramatic organic shift she could wake to one day that suggested the seemingly inescapable depths of winter had never come at all.

She would let it flow through her or not at all because, from where she stood in front of that fingerprinted jukebox, life had become so gloriously perfect in all its solitary totality and the idea of bringing someone in only to blot out the loneliness seemed absurd.

These moments of bliss are better left unanswered when faced with them being suddenly taken away.

She was a compulsive liar and she tried to destroy the beauty in everything to attempt to find it in herself. With her forehead resting on the smudged glass jukebox, staring into the limited choices of the same outdated songbook weekend after weekend, it somehow made her feel safe in the knowledge that the world turned without her attention to it, without its weight on her; it hummed and spun along to the rhythm of seventies rock and the flow of beers from strangers.

She was counting on the notion that a breeze would come through the window one evening in April, cool and sweet, bringing with it the knowledge that somehow the world works things out, weaving all the recollections tightly into a blanket that covers from start to finish. That one day spring would come and she would no longer be sleeping, and the girl she once was would be forgotten, would disappear into the iconic lyrics of another dive bar on a Saturday night.

Because we've got time. We've got so much goddamn time before we die.

NOTES

Italicized passages on Jean Piaget and memory have been quoted and adapted from "Memory (psychology)," Microsoft® Encarta® Online Encyclopedia 2007, with the exception of the passage on page 69, which has been adapted from John Daniel's 1999 essay, "The Province of Personal Narrative."

ACKNOWLEDGMENTS

First and foremost, thanks to Halli Villegas and Tightrope Books for believing in this project, and to my invaluable editor, Ari Berger, for her genius and devotion. I am also grateful to Thea Lim, Laura Meyer, and Shirarose Wilensky for last-minute copyediting heroics.

Thanks to the Toronto Arts Council and the Ontario Arts Council for their financial support, and to Zoe Whittall and Daisy Alievski, for their friendship and enthusiastic support of early versions of the manuscript.

Thanks to Michael Redhill for being my literary touchstone and friend, and to the folks at *Shameless Magazine*, *Brick* and *Descant* for all their support and (in)sanity. Thank you to the participants at Summer Literary Seminars in St. Petersburg, Russia where this novel was workshopped, and to Herb Saunders for getting me there. Thank you to Sarah Van Sinclair for being my cover star.

I am eternally grateful for the valued friendship of Mike Gibbs, Doug Glynn, Suzy Malik, Flutur Alievski and Amy Gepfert, all of whom shared an unwavering belief in me that made it possible to complete this book. Most of all I would like to thank Linda and Garry Fowles, without whom none of this would be possible.

Finally, thank you to Spencer, for doing and being everything.

ABOUT THE AUTHOR

Stacey May Fowles' writing has been published in various magazines and journals, including *Shameless Magazine, Kiss Machine, Fireweed* and *subTERRAIN*. Her non-fiction has been anthologized in the widely acclaimed *Nobody Passes: Rejecting the Rules of Gender and Conformity* and *First Person Queer*. She currently lives in Toronto. *Be Good* is her first novel.